This is what they've s... 43 LIGHT STREET ser...

On #143 LIFE LINE:

"Fasten your seat belts. Rebecca York is going to take you on a thrilling, fast-paced trip into the shadowy world of mystery and suspense and the steamy world of romance. Fantastic!"
—A. E. Ferguson, Alberta's Book Service

On #155 SHATTERED VOWS:

"Superlative suspense that will make the hairs on the back of your neck stand up and scream for help . . . a strong love story to win your heart."
—Melinda Helfer, *Romantic Times*

On #167 WHISPERS IN THE NIGHT:

"Ms. York makes you think more than twice about turning out the lights and closing your eyes, in this masterfully plotted novel of romantic suspense."
—Melinda Helfer, *Romantic Times*

On #179 ONLY SKIN DEEP:

"Another hellraiser! . . . The tension (is) at a fever pitch, with a strong romance and a cunning mystery."
—Linda Anselmi, *Romantic Times*

On #193 TRIAL BY FIRE:

"43 Light Street just keeps getting better and better! This time the devilishly clever Ms. York brews up a mind-blowing concoction of black magic and timeless romance that will fire your imagination and sear your soul."
—Melinda Helfer, *Romantic Times*

If you missed any of these earlier 43 Light Street titles, you can order them. See the ad in the back of this book.

He was no guardian angel

She realized that now. Jason Zacharias was a dangerous man—who cleverly trapped her upstairs in an isolated cottage.

On tiptoe Noel crossed the hall into the bedroom. With what little time she had, she'd find out more about who Jason really was.

In the cupboard was his duffel, and she carefully poked through its contents, trying not to change the order of his things. Jeans, shirts, a shaving kit . . . and two passport booklets with the familiar U.S. eagle crest on the outside.

The first one was issued in the name of Jason Zacharias, and he was listed as a salesman. Noel snorted. She didn't know who he was, but this man was *no* salesman.

When she opened the second booklet, the blood drained from her head. It couldn't be! It was *her* picture...and *her* signature. But her name wasn't Noel Emery. It was Noel Zacharias.

Dear Reader,

We're delighted to bring you *Hopscotch*, our most adventurous 43 Light Street book ever. Noel Emery becomes tangled in a web of international intrigue when she can't trust anyone—not even herself. And when Jason Zacharias, the bad boy from her past, shows up, she doesn't know whether to run for her life or throw herself into his arms. There are enough twists and turns in this story to keep you guessing right up until the end.

We're also happy to report that Harlequin Intrigue has renewed our lease at 43 Light Street for more books. One of the things we like best about writing a series is that we get to keep in touch with characters from previous stories. In our next book, *Cradle and All*, we're bringing back Abby Franklin and Steve Claiborne, the heroine and hero of *Life Line*, our first 43 Light Street book. Abby gives birth to their first child, but sinister forces from Steve's past come crashing in to turn their time of joy into a harrowing ordeal that has them fighting for their baby's life and their marriage.

We hope you'll join us for one of the most emotional stories we've ever written.

All our best chills and thrills,

Rebecca York
(Ruth Glick and Eileen Buckholtz)

Hopscotch

Rebecca York

Harlequin Books

TORONTO • NEW YORK • LONDON
AMSTERDAM • PARIS • SYDNEY • HAMBURG
STOCKHOLM • ATHENS • TOKYO • MILAN
MADRID • WARSAW • BUDAPEST • AUCKLAND

Harlequin Intrigue edition published February 1993

ISBN 0-373-22213-0

HOPSCOTCH

CAST OF CHARACTERS

Noel Emery—She became a pawn in a megalomaniac's dangerous game and couldn't trust anyone—not even herself.

Jason Zacharias—He was a soldier of fortune prepared to do anything to keep Noel from learning the truth.

Sir Douglas Frye—Known as the Sovereign, this ex-intelligence agent could make heads of state and CEOs dance to his tune. But he wanted even more....

Henry Marconi—His antique jewelry business was the perfect cover for his secret transactions.

Abby Franklin—Could she help Noel find her lost memories?

Flora Marconi—She wanted Noel out of the country and would pay for the trip if she would do her just one little favor....

Directory

4 3 L I G H T S T R E E T

	Room
ADVENTURES IN TRAVEL	204
BIRTH DATA, INC.	416
NOEL EMERY Paralegal Services	311
ABIGAIL FRANKLIN, Ph.D. Clinical Psychology	509
KATHRYN MARTIN, M.D.	509
O'MALLEY & O'MALLEY Detective Agency	518
LAURA ROSWELL, LL.B. Attorney at Law	311
SABRINA'S FANCY	Lobby
STRUCTURAL DESIGN GROUP	407
L. ROSSINI Superintendent	Lower Level

Prologue

Ten Years in the Past

The sun dipped behind a cloud, and the wind began to blow, lifting the fine hairs on the back of Noel Emery's neck like unseen fingers dancing along her skin.

Once more, she gave a quick half glance over her shoulder.

"Hey. You expectin' someone?" Cindy Lummos asked.

"Uh—no." Ever since the dismissal bell at Patterson High School, Noel had felt as if they were being followed. But no matter how quickly or how casually she peeked over her shoulder, she hadn't spotted anyone.

"You think Tommy D'Angelo would ask a sophomore to the Harvest Dance?" Cindy wondered. "I'll die if he takes someone else."

Noel shrugged.

"I keep forgetting. You're more interested in grades than guys."

"Majoring in boyfriends isn't going to get me a scholarship to business school."

"You're jealous."

"I've just got a lot on my mind." Noel hugged the stack of textbooks she was carrying against her chest.

Cindy's expression softened. "I know it's been tough since your dad moved out."

"We're okay." Noel scanned the sidewalk once more. Maybe it was Dad trailing her. Like that day when he'd been waiting outside school so they could talk. Only why didn't he show himself?

They had reached the small corner grocery where Mr. Dubinski let Mom run up a tab between paychecks.

"How about a soda?" Cindy asked.

Noel hesitated. She'd earned a lot more than the minimum wage helping Uncle Henry on Saturday, and she'd kept a little of the money for herself. "Okay."

Cindy touched the heart-shaped locket resting against her throat. "If you don't go to the Harvest Dance, would you—uh—mind if I keep your necklace till then?"

Noel stared at the pendant. "Well..." Really, she shouldn't have let Cindy wear it at all. Uncle Henry had just lent it to her—the way he sometimes did when he was being real nice. But he was going to want it back.

"Please."

"I guess."

"Oh, thanks! I'll treat you to a soda. And a Milky Way."

"You don't have to bribe me." Noel turned in mid-sentence. This time she thought she saw a face disappearing around the corner into the alley, and her stomach clenched. It wasn't Dad. It wasn't anyone she recognized. Quickly she brushed past her friend and hurried into the store. It was a tiny establishment with everything from soap powder to canned peas stacked on narrow floor-to-ceiling shelves.

Mr. Dubinski looked up from restocking tomato sauce as they crossed to the drink cooler. "How you girls doin'?"

"Fine."

Noel's eyes flicked to the back of the shop. What if she went out that way and ran for home? Then she tried to calm herself. Why did she assume *she* was being followed? It could just as well be some guy trying to get up his nerve to talk to Cindy.

The conversation continued without her. Something about a fight the night before in Patterson Park.

Then the door opened again, and a man stepped inside, his face carefully neutral. His head was shaved, and his hand was shoved into the pocket of a black leather jacket.

It was *him*. And he wasn't here to ask Cindy for a date. Noel knew that with a kind of awful certainty as she shrank back against her friend.

"Hey, clumsy. Watch out," Cindy hissed. "That's my toe."

"Can I help you?" Mr. Dubinski asked.

"Pack o' Camels."

"Sure." The proprietor crossed to the counter, accepted the offered bill and opened the cash drawer. While he was making the change, the stranger pulled a snub-nosed pistol out of his pocket.

"Give me the cash, Grandpa."

Mr. Dubinski turned ashen.

Cindy moaned.

Noel was incapable of making any sort of sound. This time, when she squeezed back against her friend, there was no protest.

"Hurry it up, ol' man! Put the cash in a paper bag."

The skinhead had heard Cindy; the weapon swung in their direction. "Hold it right there." For a fraction of a second, the hood's narrowed gaze darted from one girl to the other and back again. It came to rest on the jewel-studded heart nestled in the hollow of Cindy's throat. "I'll have that, too."

From the corner of her eye, Noel saw Mr. Dubinski reach below the counter, but the thug sensed the movement, too. Whirling, he fired off two shots.

With a strangled sound, Mr. Dubinski toppled backward.

Screaming, Cindy pushed past Noel and dashed toward the exit. She never reached the door. Another shot reverberated in the enclosed space, and she slumped to the uneven floorboards. Leaning over her, the robber snapped the slim gold chain, yanked the locket free, and stuffed it into his jacket pocket.

Noel was backing farther into the corner when he rounded on her. He had just killed two people. She was probably next. However, instead of shooting, he took a step toward her.

Noel's brain was barely functioning. The only thing she knew was that she wasn't going to let him touch her without a fight. The hand that hung limply at her side wrapped itself around a can.

All his attention was focused on her, so that he didn't see the light in back of him change subtly. Then the door opened again, this time very quietly. In a blur of motion, a figure sprang out of the daylight, hit the gunman and slammed him back against the counter.

Reflexively Noel threw the can, striking her target square in the shoulder.

"Jeez!" An exclamation of shock and dismay burst from the killer.

The two men began a desperate fight for possession of the gun.

Noel sagged against the cooler, unable to wrest her eyes from the struggle. The tiny part of her mind that still worked recognized the newcomer. Jason Zacharias. A tough guy from school who'd taken her out a couple of times and then dropped her.

The gun went off again, and the bullet slammed into a can of tomato sauce, splattering Noel. Seconds later, the weapon skated across the black-and-white tiles and slid under the counter. Then a foot kicked out, hitting one of the shelves, and cans rained down on the floor, rolling every which way.

Ignoring everything but each other, the men traded punches and grunts, but gradually it looked as if Jason was winning. Finally he brought the killer down with one last punch. The only sound in the room was Jason's agonized breathing.

Noel watched him push himself up and stand, swaying as he looked down at the unconscious man on the floor. Staggering to the counter, he leaned his elbows on it, panting. His denim jacket was ripped. His dark hair hung in his face.

After a moment he raised his head and stared at Noel. His face was battered, and his left eye was discolored and swelling shut.

She gasped. So did he. "Oh, God. You're hit," he croaked.

Jason swayed toward her. Three years older than she, he was supposed to be bad news. He didn't look rebellious now. He looked scared.

She followed the direction of his gaze. Splashes of red marred her mint green sweater, and momentarily she didn't understand what she was seeing. "No—I'm—it's just tomatoes—"

His hand connected with the soft knit sweater, touching the damp red splotches. It came to rest over the spot where her heart thumped wildly in her chest. She and

Jason stared at each other, neither of them moving, neither of them breaking the contact. Then he seemed to remember where they were and why. In slow motion, he brought his fingers to his lips. "Yeah, tomato sauce."

His words broke the spell. "Cindy," Noel whispered. "And Mr. Dubinski."

He turned and crossed to the girl sprawled on the floor, kneeling down beside her.

"Is she—?"

"Dead." After checking, he issued the same diagnosis for the proprietor.

A wordless sound of anguish trickled from Noel's throat, and she started to shake. Jason was beside her then, folding his arms around her, keeping her safe. He'd held her close a couple of times before, when he'd taken her home after a movie and made her head spin with his kisses. Now only his strong arms cradling her shaking body kept her from sinking to the floor.

Jason held her tightly against his street-tough frame. Then she felt his grasp change as he looked down into her bewildered face.

"Noel. Pull yourself together." His voice was low and urgent.

Reality had narrowed to Jason's muscular body sheltering hers. She moaned in protest when he thrust her away from himself, shaking her shoulders. "You can't go to pieces now."

Her gaze bounced from Mr. Dubinski to Cindy. "She...she...said she was going to die if Tommy didn't ask her to the dance...." She trailed off on a sob.

Jason's hands tightened on her shoulders. "Stop it! Before that guy wakes up, you've got to call the cops."

She stared up into his deep brown eyes, so dark they were almost black. "Please. Can't you do it?"

"If they find me here, they'll think I was with him."

"But you...you saved me. I'm going to tell them that."

"No. Tell them how you threw the can. Say you don't know who came in or where he went."

Before she could answer, he crossed the store, stepped over the cans and left.

Chapter One

The man in the rented room narrowed his eyes against the morning sunlight. With a practiced hand, he reached to adjust the custom-designed lens of his video camera. Beyond the streaked window of Marconi, Ltd., the proprietor was getting out trays of rings and bracelets. An innocent enough activity, unless you knew the real story behind Henry Marconi's success.

Six months ago Sovereign Enterprises had rented the upstairs apartment across from the little shop. For five months the shabby rooms had remained vacant, even though the rent had been paid promptly by a downtown bank before the first of each month.

Then, at the beginning of the previous week, the man had gotten his orders. Late the next evening, he'd moved in so unobtrusively that the landlady, Mrs. Potts, hadn't even known he was there until she heard the water running in the pipes. After a brief conversation at the door of his room, she'd kept out of his way. Which was exactly what he wanted.

Mostly he left his post at night, coming and going with the silence and measured pace of a nocturnal animal. Keeping his business private was an old habit. This time he had the added burden of making sure he didn't draw attention to himself in the neighborhood.

Of course, that wasn't too difficult in Fells Point, a working-class community experiencing the mixed blessings of gentrification. His seaman's jacket, short haircut and tough features would have been at home in any of the older bars. And the faded scar on his left cheek only added a touch of verisimilitude to the picture.

He watched through the video camera lens as Marconi swallowed a couple of pills and stood holding the glass. Then the old man glanced toward the window. Was he expecting someone?

The watcher followed Marconi's gaze down the sidewalk and saw a woman turn the corner off Broadway. At first, her walk interested him more than her face. He'd spent years studying people, gauging their state of mind from their body language. Her hesitant stride told him she wished she were somewhere else. The tight fingers wrapped around the strap of her shoulder bag reinforced the impression.

Then she pushed her long, dark hair aside, and in the space of a heartbeat he felt as if he'd been socked in the gut.

Noel. It was Noel.

Jason Zacharias felt his heart stop and then start to pound. Unable to move, unable to tear his gaze away, he stared at her, drinking in details. She was older, more polished. More beautiful. Still, he'd know that upturned nose, those large blue eyes and that sensual mouth anywhere. Against his will, he was swamped with sensations that had burned themselves into his memory. The warm, sweet scent of her body. The feel of her lips against his. The way the silky strands of her hair curled around his fingers.

With a low growl, he pulled himself out of the reverie.

He and Noel had connected in another life. She wasn't supposed to exist in this one, too. And she sure as hell wasn't supposed to come walking into the video he was taping.

Jason closed his eyes and called upon one of the Oriental relaxation exercises he'd learned in a village outside Shanghai. After a minute, his heartbeat slowed and his mind cleared. He willed Noel to keep moving down the sidewalk, to walk off the set. But she didn't. She paused and straightened her shoulders, then turned in between the dusty show windows of Marconi, Ltd.

"Damn. Double damn." The curse that went all the way back to Jason's childhood slipped out between his teeth. He sat rigid, forgetting the relaxation technique, forgetting to adjust the lens while the proprietor let her in. Then, remembering who was going to be looking at the tape, he reached to correct the focus. But the emotions he'd worked so hard to suppress still churned.

What the hell was *she* doing here?

NOEL ROLLED HER ACHING shoulders, stretched, and looked toward the grime-streaked window of the antique-jewelry shop, surprised that the sun was setting. She and Uncle Henry had been working almost all day.

"I think we can get one more tray done this evening," Henry said.

Noel turned to him with concern. His large hands were trembling slightly as he set a velvet-lined box of rings on the counter. Trying to conceal a grimace, he settled heavily back into the desk chair she'd brought out front when she'd seen him swaying on his feet. Once he'd been a roly-poly giant who had a ready quip for every situation. He was still tall, but his shoulders were stooped and the pale skin of his face hung in loose folds. At the moment, his brow was beaded with perspiration.

"Maybe we should call it a day," Noel said quietly. "Tomorrow's Sunday. We can work till dinner again if you want."

"But you've got to be back at your secretary's job on Monday."

"I'm not a secretary anymore."

"Oh, pardon me, Miss Paralegal. What do you make, twenty thou a year?" Henry didn't bother to scrub the sarcasm from his voice.

"More than that," Noel said evenly.

"You used to love working for me on the weekends and in the summer. And you know as much about antique jewelry as some of the experts. Are you really turning down the chance to go into business for yourself so you can run somebody's law office?"

"Not *somebody*. Laura Roswell, and she depends on me." Noel took her lower lip between her teeth. Henry looked down at his gnarled hands. They'd had this discussion before. What always went unspoken was that he'd been out of the country on an extended buying trip more than once when she'd needed aid and comfort. Now he was the one in trouble, and she was torn between old loyalties and new.

"I'm sorry. That wasn't fair," the weary man acknowledged. "Are you annoyed because I don't want you setting up shop here? Really, this isn't a good location. Not enough traffic."

"Uncle Henry, please. That's not it."

"Well, whatever you decide, the stock will be yours. You can keep the pieces you want to wear or sell everything off, if you like. But I don't want to die without having everything in order. Do you understand?"

Noel put her hand on his shoulder. She wanted to tell him he was going to be around for years. They both knew that would be a lie. Since he'd been a teenager, Henry Marconi had joshingly called his cigarettes "coffin nails." Six months ago he'd stopped joking about what they'd done to his lungs.

"If you're feeling up to it, maybe we can get through another tray before we quit," Noel said.

He gave her a grateful look and selected a small antique ring. Then he put the jeweler's loop back to his eye. "Number 437. Gold, cameo with small round diamonds, size 5, $525."

Noel picked up the pen and notebook she'd been using to record the inventory. At Laura's office, all the files were in the computer, but Uncle Henry had told her often enough that he didn't trust information stored as electrical impulses.

After finishing with the cameo, he went on to number 438, a lion's head with emerald eyes.

Noel dutifully entered the data, but she only needed part of her mind to do the job. She was thinking that life rarely worked out the way you expected.

AFTER WATCHING through his camera lens for eight straight hours, Jason had a little better idea of how Noel fit into the picture. She was helping Marconi take inventory, although she hadn't been mentioned in his briefing folder. Too bad the construction crew renovating the shop a couple of doors down was keeping him from picking up any useful audio from the directional mike. Or maybe that was lucky, too. He wouldn't be called upon to interpret the conversation later. When you worked for someone who thought he was God, it was better if the real deity threw in a wild card now and then.

Jason sighed, considering once again the chain of events that had brought him into the employ of Sir Douglas Frye, the Scottish laird who styled himself the Sovereign. When Jason had left Baltimore, he'd vowed never to come back. For most of the past ten years, he'd kept the promise. At first, his goal had been to put as much distance as possible between himself and a city that considered him expendable. He'd been everywhere from Latin America to the Far East, much of the travel courtesy of the U.S. Marines. Then he'd discovered rather bitterly that you never knew what kind of twist life was going to take. He'd free-lanced for a couple of years before signing on with Frye. His new employer had taken full advantage of his military training, his language abilities and his reputation for ruthlessness.

Eyes narrowing, Jason shifted his attention back to the shop and its occupants. Was this one more test Frye's new right-hand man was going to have to pass to prove his loyalty? And what exactly was the challenge going to be?

HALFWAY THROUGH the last tray of rings, Noel looked up and felt her chest squeeze painfully as she took in the gray color of her uncle's skin and the rigid set of his jaw.

"Do you need one of your pain pills?"

When he nodded tightly, Noel went to fetch a glass of water and the small plastic bottle.

"You know, it's been a pretty long day," she said after he swallowed a yellow capsule. "Why don't we start up again in the morning?"

"I guess maybe you're right."

"Then I'll just put this batch in the safe." Noel picked up the velvet-lined tray and started for the office at the back of the shop.

Before she reached the door, she heard her uncle clear his throat. "Honey, I don't know why you put up with me."

She turned halfway around, not quite facing him. "I guess I have to. You're all the family I have left."

"Not for long."

"Don't say that. Maybe you have a lot longer than you think."

"Maybe." The look on his face said otherwise. Noel hurried off to the back room. She and Uncle Henry had never been all that good at putting their feelings into words, but probably he'd like a chance to talk. What if she invited him back to her apartment for supper?

As Noel opened the safe, she heard the bell over the door jingle. It was followed by the sound of male voices. Her hand tightened on the tray of rings. Only three people had come in to buy any jewelry during the day. Now, when they were about to close and Uncle Henry was exhausted, he had to wait on a customer.

Anxious to take some of the burden from her uncle, Noel set the box of rings on the desk beside the safe and hurried back to the showroom. On the way, she rearranged her features. It was never politic to let a customer see that you were annoyed.

Noel grabbed the curtain that separated the front from the back of the shop—and stopped in her tracks. Two men were facing her uncle. Two men holding guns with strange, long barrels.

As her gaze careened from the men to the weapons, she froze—body, hands and can-I-help-you smile.

It was several seconds before Noel could move. Very quietly, her heart pounding in her throat, she began to back up. When she was several feet from the door, she turned. The phone was on the deck. If she could just call the emergency number before—

A rough hand on her shoulder made the air congeal in her lungs.

"Come on in and join the party."

The hand yanked her back into the front room. And into a time warp. She was sixteen years old again. In Mr. Dubinski's grocery store. Blood roared in Noel's ears as she tried to make sense of the scene from her nightmares. It had all happened a long time ago. Why was it coming back now?

No, she had it wrong. This time there were two guns and two men. One was tall and skeletal, and he looked as if he were getting ready to squash a grub he'd found under a rock. The other was medium height, medium weight. If he hadn't been pointing a gun at her stomach, Noel probably would have walked past him on the street without a second thought. But the gun made all the difference.

An old man leaned against the counter, his hand trembling where it rested on the glass case. For a second, Noel's mind continued to play tricks. When he looked up, she expected to see Mr. Dubinski's frightened face. Then her mind put the pieces of the picture into the right order, and she knew it was Uncle Henry.

"Over there, doll."

Numbly Noel moved to the other end of the counter, pressing her hips and legs against the ancient wood to keep herself upright.

Her eyes slid to her uncle, then snapped back to the taller gunman as he began to speak.

"I guess you know what we've come for," he said in a voice that was all the more deadly for its quiet assumption of compliance.

"No," Henry Marconi denied.

"Don't play games with us."

"Who sent you?"

"Any game that gets played here, we set the rules."

"But—"

An arm whipped out, and a fist cracked into Henry Marconi's face. He groaned and sagged toward the floor. As he went down, Noel tried to rush toward him. A hand grabbed her by the hair and slammed her against the counter.

The scream of pain that tore from her lips made Henry's head jerk up.

"I think we've got his attention," the man holding Noel remarked.

"No! Leave her alone."

"Why should we?" the man who was in charge asked.

"She just came in to help me with the inventory. She doesn't know anything."

"But you do."

Henry licked dry lips.

The skeleton hauled him to his feet. He stood swaying and panting, his face the color of dirty putty.

"Don't do this to him. Can't you see he's sick?" Noel pleaded.

"Keep your mouth shut," her captor growled, then turned back to Uncle Henry. "Don't waste any more of our time."

Silent communication passed between the intruders. Then the one who still held Noel swept his hand roughly, insinuatingly down the front of her body.

"No. Please," she choked out as she tried to cringe away from the dirty, invading touch.

He held her back tightly against his front, a little chuckle bubbling from his mouth as he continued the exploration. "Nice."

Noel began to shake as one nightmare was blended with another. She'd been grabbed like this before. Held. Touched. And then it had gotten much worse.

Uncle Henry was looking at her, his face twisted in pain. She shrank away from his misery as much as anything else.

For a terrible moment there was only silence and the frantic pounding of blood in her ears.

The hush was broken by the other man. "Where is the shipment?"

"I'll give you anything you want. Just let her go." Defeat, anguish, fear all mingled in the old man's answer.

"No tricks."

"Turn her loose first." Henry's voice was stronger now.

"You're not in a position to bargain."

"Turn her loose."

The skeleton nodded. There was a little sigh of regret as the hands dropped from Noel's body. She stumbled away and crossed her arms protectively over her chest.

"Stop stalling. Get the stuff."

The old man shuffled toward the cash register. Then he was behind the counter, reaching down and fumbling for something.

"Hurry up."

"Got to unlock the box."

She had to get away, and the only place to hide was inside her own mind. Noel stood with her eyes glazed, barely paying attention to what was going on around her until she heard the rasp of metal against metal. The sound set her teeth on edge, and her eyes darted to her uncle, crouched below the level of the counter. All she could see was the bald top of his head.

He was getting something out of the box. It wasn't locked. She'd opened it once by mistake, and she knew what was in it. A gun. The gun she'd begged Uncle Henry to get rid of. And now it was all happening again—

"No!" Noel screamed as she surged toward the counter. There was only one thought in her mind. If he pulled out the gun, he was a dead man. And she had to stop him.

The cry and the sudden, urgent movement were a total surprise to the man in back of her, but he recovered quickly. Before Noel reached the display case, a curse exploded from his lips, and he lunged toward her.

Chapter Two

Jason Zacharias's assignment had been very specific. "Stay inconspicuous. Videotape any activity in the jewelry shop. Under no circumstances interfere with the course of events."

He had never disobeyed a direct order from the Sovereign. For forty-five seconds after the men who entered the shop had pulled their guns, he stood behind the camera, watching the action as the blood had drained from Henry Marconi's face and the old man had backed up against the counter until there was no more room to maneuver. Then one of the men stepped through the curtain and yanked Noel back into the shop.

At that moment, Jason stopped thinking about orders and consequences. Grabbing his gun, he pounded down the stairs, cursing the interval when he couldn't see what was going on in the little shop of horrors.

He saw a flash of movement inside the store as he dashed across the street. Above the construction noise down the block, he heard two shots in rapid succession. His own semiautomatic was in his outstretched hand.

He pulled open the door and stopped dead in his tracks. Marconi lay against the wall in back of the counter. It looked as if he'd gone for a concealed weapon and fired upward through the display case, hitting both of the intruders. However, one of them had also taken care of Marconi on the way down.

Dead. The crooks and the proprietor were dead. He didn't have to feel for a pulse to know. However, at the moment, the only occupant of the room he cared about was the woman who lay facedown, arms at her sides, several feet in front of the shorter thug.

His heart blocking his windpipe, Jason stared at her. When she groaned and moved one arm, something seemed to break apart in his chest. Three long strides, one of them across the taller thug, brought him to her side. Kneeling, he touched the bloody lump at the back of her head. As practiced fingers determined the source of the injury, he let out a long sigh of relief. As far as he could tell, the wound had been caused by a blow. Probably from the butt of a gun.

His eyes flicked to the man who'd had his obscene hands on Noel. He'd been busy trying to crack her skull, which was why he hadn't been ready to return Marconi's fire. If luck had been with her, she'd gone down a fraction of a second before the shooting started.

Carefully he rolled Noel to her back and felt for a pulse in her neck, breathing another sigh of relief when he found it shallow but steady. Next his hands moved quickly and surely over her body as he searched for other damage, remembering to breathe only when he didn't find any bullet wounds.

His fingers drifted upward to her cheek in a touch that was more a caress than an attempt to get any more medical information. For a moment, he was caught and held by a fairy-tale memory. Of the two of them together.

"Noel?"

She didn't respond.

"Noel?" He might have shaken her, but he didn't want to take a chance with the head injury. How hard had the bastard hit her?

He stared at her ashen face. Even in this condition, she was beautiful. And so damned innocent looking.

"You should have learned to stay out of trouble," he grated. "What the hell are you doing here?"

Was it his imagination, or had her lids fluttered? "How much do you know about Marconi's dirty little export business? Are you in on the deal? How much is he paying you?"

She didn't answer. Before he could ask another useless question, he heard the wail of a siren. It was a long way off, but it was getting louder.

The sound brought him back to reality and his own precarious situation. Had someone seen him on the street, or heard the shots? His gaze swung from Noel to the scene of destruction. He had it all on tape, because the camera was still running.

He cursed. He was on the footage, too. He'd have to take care of that. And think of a damn good reason why the camera had stopped recording at such a crucial moment.

As he looked around the shop, he grimaced at the sight—and at its eerie parallel to the past. He'd come in on a scene like this once before. Then he'd been a two-bit punk afraid of the cops. Now he was a trained professional with a job to do.

Quickly he checked for evidence that anyone besides the victims had been in the shop. Then, carefully, he gathered Noel up into his arms and strode toward the back door.

SHE CAME SLOWLY UP, up through layers of deep sleep.

"Noel? Noel?"

Jason was calling her name. She smiled. Jason. She knew his voice. He was here again. Last time...

Last time...she tried to hold on to the memory, but it slithered away from her.

"Noel? Wake up. Please, sweetheart."

Jason. But it couldn't be him. He was long ago and far away. It had to be the one with the bald head. The one who had shot Mr. Dubinski.

Whimpering, she tried to shrink away.

"Noel. Stay with me, Noel. You've got to wake up."

She wanted to flee back through the light blue haze behind her closed lids to the sheltering cobalt and then to the midnight depths where no harm could reach her. The insistent voice and the hand gripping her shoulder wouldn't let her escape.

"Come on, Noel. I know you're in there."

Her eyelids fluttered, and she grimaced at the sudden brightness.

"Does the light hurt?"

"Yes," she whispered.

Magically the glare no longer shone in her eyes.

Still it was difficult to make out the face hovering above her. She struggled to bring it into focus. The first thing she saw was a pair of dark, almost black eyes fringed by long lashes. She knew those eyes. She could never forget those eyes.

"Jason."

"Yes."

"Why...did...you leave?"

He didn't answer. The stark look on his face made her want to reach out toward him, but her arms were too heavy to lift.

Head throbbing, she sank back against the pillows, exhausted by the brief conversation.

She wasn't sure how much time passed before she spoke again. "Wh-what are you doing here?"

"A job."

When he moved away, panic grabbed her. Then he was back, laying a cool cloth across her pounding forehead. The hand holding the cloth touched her cheek, bringing her more fully awake.

She blinked. "Where am I?"

"My room."

"How?" Talking was a tremendous effort.

"What happened in the shop?"

"I—" An image skirted at the frayed edge of her brain. It wouldn't take on substance, but a feeling of terrible loss swept over her. Her eyes searched his, pleading. "Help me."

His face twisted as if some bitter pain had seeped into his soul. He came down beside her, taking her in his arms, holding her. Keeping her safe. How long ago had it been since he'd held her like this? A vivid memory of his embrace, of his kiss, enveloped her. Was that a dream? Or was this?

He stroked her shoulders and the back of her neck. She buried her face against his chest, needing his comfort, content simply to exist in his arms.

It didn't last.

He growled something she couldn't catch as he lowered her back against the pillows. Sad, confused, hurting, she felt tears leaking from behind her closed lids.

His arm was behind her head, lifting her up. Then a glass touched against her lips, and she took a swallow of orange juice. It helped moisten her dry mouth.

Jason set the glass on the bed stand. "Were you working for Marconi?"

"Sometimes."

"Doing what?"

"Things...."

"What were you doing there today?"

"He's sick." She paused to gather enough strength to answer. "He...he...wants me to have the jewelry. But he can't tell me he loves me." The pain swelled like a balloon in her head, making it impossible to think. She pressed her hand to her temple.

"Noel. What is it? Sweetheart, what's wrong?" He was beside her again, his fingers digging into her shoulders as if he could anchor her to the here and now. But the blue haze wafted toward her, and she reached out toward it.

"Noel—"

She was afraid, and she fled from him as much as from the pain. She had thought he was here to help her. Now she sensed that wasn't true.

Some time later Noel opened her eyes and blinked as she took in her surroundings. A tall, muscular man was standing with his back to her, looking out the window. His hands were wedged into the back pockets of a pair of worn jeans.

She didn't know who he was, and panic clawed at her chest. Her eyes flicked from the rigid shoulders to the unfamiliar room. A bed. A chest. A lamp. Several black cases sitting by the door. Packed luggage. Not hers. At least, she didn't think so.

What was she doing here? What did he want with her? Stealthily she tried to push herself off the bed, tried to get away. She didn't have the strength.

When he heard her flop back against the pillow, he whirled to face her. She found herself staring up into eyes so dark they were nearly black. She knew those eyes. She would never forget those eyes. Jason. But it couldn't be Jason.

She said his name anyway. Just in case.

His fingers gently stroked the hair back from her face. "How do you feel?"

"Bad."

"I need to find out more about Henry Marconi."

"Uncle Henry."

"Yes. His export jewelry business."

"Export?" She moved her tongue against the inside of her lips. "Why does my mouth taste like orange juice?"

His eyes narrowed. "I gave you a drink. Don't you remember?"

She tried to shake her head and winced at the stab of pain. "What happened? Where am I?"

"In my room. We were talking a few minutes ago."

"We were?"

He swore under his breath. "I think I'd better get you to the hospital."

"Am I sick?"

"Everything's going to be all right."

She smiled with relief. If Jason Zacharias said everything was going to be all right, it must be true.

THE INTRUDER WORE a white coat over a slightly rumpled oxford-cloth shirt and gray slacks. He walked quickly, purposefully down the dimly lit hospital corridor—an excellent imitation of a physician stopping by one of the wards to check on a patient.

It was five-thirty in the morning. The graveyard shift, so to speak. He'd picked the time carefully. The day staff wouldn't arrive for an hour. The night staff was overworked and tired.

He didn't need to stop at the nurses' station to find Room 23C. He'd been briefed on that and every other detail he needed to know.

A few moments later, he stepped into the girl's room.

Her name was Noel Emery. Not that it made any difference to him.

As he'd expected, she was sleeping, her face pale but peaceful. Her breathing regular.

From one of the deep pockets in his coat, he took a hypodermic and removed the cap. Then he reached for her arm. A sedative was risky for someone in her condition, but that wasn't his problem. Quickly he stabbed the needle into her flesh, closing his hand over her mouth to stifle her little moan of protest.

While he waited for the drug to take effect, he carefully took her handprint on a sheet of specially coated paper. Then he pulled on surgical gloves and tipped her head to the side, inspecting the place where her scalp had been stitched a few hours earlier.

With sharp little scissors, he snipped the surgical threads, pulled them carefully out, and opened the wound. A sterile wad of gauze stanched the flow of blood.

Deftly he performed a procedure that wasn't in any medical textbook. Then he carefully sewed the incision together again, using the same pattern of six stitches that he'd originally found.

When he was done, he swabbed the area with alcohol and inspected his handiwork.

Perfect. Or so close to the original that no one was going to see any difference.

It wasn't until that moment he realized perspiration was beading his forehead. He wiped it away with his sleeve before stepping into the hall again and heading quickly for the exit.

NOEL HAD BEEN at Abby Franklin's house for three days now. Three frustrating days. Stopping on the garden path, she tried to summon a feeling of calm. In the hospital, it had taken the staff and her friends days to pull her out of the deadening mist. Oblivion had been a comfort, a security blanket to wrap around her wounded mind. Because when she came back to reality, it would be too terrifying to face. Again.

Chaos.

No. She wouldn't let the swirling confusion take her.

For just a moment, a thought flickered at the edge of her awareness. Something important that she had to remember.

Before this had happened—

Then someone came around the corner, and Noel froze.

"There you are."

It was her friend, Abby Franklin, carrying two glasses of orange juice.

Since Noel had awakened two weeks ago, she'd craved orange juice. Which was strange, because she'd never had a passion for the stuff before. But then there were many things you could call strange. If that's how you wanted to interpret the present situation.

Abby's husband, Steve, was on the Eastern Shore deciding whether to buy a small airport and charter-flight service. And Dr. Franklin had said she'd like some company. That was convenient for Noel. If you had a couple of screws loose, it was just as well to be staying with a friend who was a psychologist.

Abby, who was five months pregnant, handed Noel the glass of juice.

"How are you feeling?"

Noel took in a deep breath and let it out slowly. "Okay. What about you? Is taking care of a disabled houseguest getting to be too much?"

"Nonsense. How are you really feeling?"

Noel slid a finger up the side of the glass. "Scared."

"Are you disoriented again?"

"I guess it shows."

Abby put an arm around her shoulder. Together they walked back to the house.

"I've told you, it takes a while to get over a severe head injury," Abby said as they reached the patio.

"But you'd think I'd remember my uncle getting shot, wouldn't you?"

Abby shook her head. "The shooting is exactly the thing I'd expect you to blank out. It was too traumatic."

A familiar panicky feeling clawed at Noel's insides. "I don't even know how I got to the hospital."

"Somebody must have come in and decided you needed medical attention."

For just a moment, she pictured a pair of brown eyes so dark they were almost black. "Why doesn't he contact me?"

"Who? Are you starting to remember that part?"

A name hovered on the tip of Noel's tongue, but she knew she was only conjuring up a fantasy. A guardian angel from her past. "No. I guess I keep assuming a guy picked me up and carried me to his car. Or a lady weight lifter."

"It looks like he didn't want to get any deeper involved," Abby suggested.

Noel grimaced. "Yeah. I can understand that. But I hate walking around in a daze like this. I hate being terrified every time I hear footsteps in back of me." Gingerly she reached up, pushed her long hair aside and touched the line of stitches at the back of her head. That tender, vulnerable spot had become the physical symbol of what had happened to her. Sighing, she sat down in one of the patio chairs and set the juice on the table.

Abby took another chair. "The disorientation will go away, and your memory will come back," she said softly.

"When? I'm no good to Laura. She's going to have to hire another paralegal if she wants to keep her office going. I'm no good to the police. I can't tell them any more about what happened in my uncle's shop than they can figure out from looking at the crime scene. I'm no good to anyone. And I don't like being dependent!"

Abby let her rant on until Noel came smack up against the subject she'd been avoiding and abruptly stopped.

"Tell me," Abby urged. "Don't be scared. Whatever it is, I've heard it before."

"It's not what you think." Noel gulped. "This word keeps popping into my head. Chaos."

"That's not so odd. Maybe it's a metaphor for how you feel."

"Okay. I'll tell you the rest of it. The police say I was in the back at the safe, since I'm the only one who didn't get shot. That one of the men probably came in and hit me over the head before I knew what was happening. But what if—" Noel shrugged helplessly. How did you explain a feeling of dread you couldn't back up with facts or even memories? "What if. . . someone thinks I know what happened? What if they want to shut me up?"

"Honey, Dan Cassidy has been all over the case. As far as he can tell, it was only a robbery attempt gone bad."

Noel nodded. Dan Cassidy was the assistant state's attorney who was engaged to Sabrina Barkley, one of her best friends from 43 Light Street.

"A lot of people knew your uncle was winding down his business. He was supposed to have sold off some stock for cash. Two local thugs thought they could share the wealth."

"I guess." Noel turned away so Abby couldn't see her face. She knew it mirrored the sick feeling that washed over her whenever she tried to penetrate the dead zone in her mind.

"EN GARDE."

"Allez."

Sir Douglas Frye went on the attack. Sword extended, he lunged at his adversary. The taller man, who would have been more at ease with a bayonet, gave ground, moving backward down the piste.

A smile flickered on Sir Douglas's thin lips. He might be in his sixties, but he still had the speed and finesse to challenge someone half his age.

The clash of steel meeting steel sang out in the bracing Highland air. He knew the younger man was testing his teacher's skill more forcefully than he ever had before. Then, with a surprise countermove, the novice went on the attack with a riposte, a quick thrust after the parry.

Sir Douglas fought off the attack with a series of lightning-swift moves. In many ways, he and his opponent couldn't be more different. Or more alike.

Managing to keep his movements graceful, he searched for a sign of weakness he could use to his advantage even as he fell back farther. Adrenaline pumped through his veins, and a film of moisture slicked his brow. Wielding power on a vast global scale had its gratifications, but there was nothing like the thrill of hand-to-hand combat when you looked into the eye of an adversary who had fought to the death many times.

To his astonishment, the point of his opponent's foil touched the front of his protective shirt.

"Touché."

"Good strike, laddie," he congratulated. His pupil was a quick learner, perhaps too quick.

"You were thinking about something else for a moment. I took advantage of that."

"Aye. I was."

In former times, fencing had been a deadly enterprise. Now it was an aristocratic sport. Yet there were ways to make the contest more exciting than the standard rules allowed. Today, both men were wearing only part of the protective garb usually prescribed. Neither had a face mask, because Sir Douglas had always enjoyed seeing the fear in an opponent's eyes. Both on and off the piste. Just once he'd like the satisfaction of seeing that in Jason Zacharias's eyes. He suspected he never would.

"I was thinking about the delivery you made for me on your way back from Baltimore."

"It was nice to see Cairo again."

"No problem with customs, I assume."

"Money in the right hands does wonders."

"One of my guiding principles." Frye continued in a disarming voice, "Speaking of Baltimore, I sent the tape of the jewelry shop in for analysis."

Jason Zacharias didn't flick an eyelash or change his position in the slightest. Commendable, the Sovereign thought. Either Zacharias was absolutely what he appeared to be—a loyal agent who'd just completed a couple of important assignments—or a consummate actor. And that was precisely the problem. There was something about the whole Marconi incident that didn't ring quite true.

Sir Douglas Frye had learned to pay attention to his hunches. He'd also learned to ask the right questions in the right way, to feint and parry just as he would on the court and to judge the flutter of an expression across a face so that he got the answers he needed even if the subject didn't know he was giving anything away.

But no one else had ever perplexed the Sovereign as much as Jason Zacharias. Not his former colleagues in MI6. Not the Eastern Bloc operatives he'd hounded. Not the desperate politicians and captains of industry who'd become his clients. None of them was as worthy an adversary as this boy from a working-class Greek neighborhood who had grown up to be as dangerous a fencing opponent as he was a back-alley fighter.

To test the depth of Zacharias's impassiveness, Frye began another parry.

"En garde."

"Allez."

This time he pressed the attack with all the skill he'd acquired in forty-five years of fierce competition. He held off the other man's victory for several minutes, but he couldn't deflect the blade that slipped past his defenses yet again and scored a hit over his heart.

He put down his foil, grabbed a thick towel and wiped the perspiration from his head and neck. "Most men who work for me have the good sense to let me win, laddie."

Jason laughed. "We both like to win."

"Aye. By the way, there wasn't any problem with the analysis."

"I wasn't expecting one."

"Still, it's verra like Nixon, don't you think? With his eighteen-minute gap."

Jason chuckled. "Trust your suspicious mind! But I don't have a Rosemary Woods willing to swear that she caused an erasure by stepping on the wrong Dictaphone pedal."

"You've got your Noel Emery."

"Oh?"

"The niece."

"Is that her name?"

"Aye." Frye strolled over to the bar sheltered under a striped canopy. "We both deserve a wee bit of refreshment."

"Yes."

The laird of the castle poured out two Waterford glasses of Glenfiddich. The premium Scotch was one of the compensations God had given his native country to make up for the beastly weather and rugged terrain more suitable for sheep than people.

Jason took a sip of the 101-proof liquor. "I'm getting to appreciate this stuff."

"We'll make a Scot o' you yet."

"You can try." He gave Frye a direct look. "For the record, it's not an eighteen-minute gap. I simply ran out of tape. I'm sorry. Marconi left the shop at five-thirty every day, and it was already after six. I assumed the show was almost over for the evening."

"An understandable mistake."

"Luckily you saw the crucial part. The two thugs coming in. One of them manhandling the girl. Marconi going for his gun."

Jason's face gave nothing away. "He was quite a marksman."

"From his old Green Beret days. It didn't help him any." Frye made one of his rapid subject changes. "What's the status of the lass now?"

Jason repeated the information he'd submitted in his coded fax report. "She had a concussion from the blow to her head. She's out of the hospital now. When I left Baltimore, she still didn't remember anything."

"Probably to our advantage."

"Yes."

"And the two ruffians? Who were they?"

"Local talent. At least, that's what the police and the state's attorney's office think."

"Your investigation confirms that?" Frye probed.

"Yes."

"I don't like coincidences."

"I know."

"I did some checking on the lass."

Jason set his glass down carefully. "And?"

"Father moved out of the house when she was fifteen. The next year, she was in a neighborhood green-grocers that was robbed. Her friend and the proprietor were killed. Another customer came in and saved her life."

"Who?"

"She was too distraught to get his name."

"What happened to the perp?" Jason inquired.

"Died in jail before he came to trial."

"Interesting."

"Jail can be a rather violent place."

Jason gave him a hard look. "Like the stockade."

"It's difficult to forget one's own sordid past."

"How would you know? You don't have one."

"Ah, but there's my ancestry. The Fryes didn't always live in Castle Lockwood. I think I know you well enough to tell you how the family got their start up the ladder to affluence."

"A royal land grant?"

Sir Douglas laughed. "Hardly. My great-great-great-grandfather turned in an uppity, redheaded witch to the authorities and got a fat reward—and her confiscated cottage. When he moved her wee bed, he found a bag of silver coins buried in the dirt floor. He used them to buy livestock."

"That makes a good story."

"Believe it or not, as you please." Standing up, the Sovereign walked to the massive stone staircase, turned back toward Jason and fixed him with a thoughtful look.

"Verra odd, you don't know her."

"The witch?"

"The Emery lass. She went to the same high school you did. Patterson."

"I wasn't there much." He grinned. "That's why they kicked me out."

"You managed to get an education, anyway."

"It's not what you'd call conventional."

"Miss Emery went on to secretarial school. Now she's a paralegal and had been considering taking a law degree."

"Good for her."

"I've got some more rubbish, if you're interested," Frye said.

"No harm in sifting through dirt if there's a chance it will yield platinum."

"Aye. You're better than a metal detector. That's one of the reasons I recruited you."

"And because I'm a better shot than Henry Marconi, I suppose."

"You have a lot of talents. I was lucky the Marine Corps dispensed with your services."

"A polite way to put it. But I think the association has been to our mutual advantage."

"Definitely."

"What were you going to tell me about Miss Emery?"

"There was an interesting incident four years ago involving her married employer. A man named Gilmore."

"She was having an affair with him?" Jason asked as if he weren't very interested.

"He may have raped her."

Frye watched carefully, wondering if he caught a flicker of emotion on Zacharias's face. But the man's mask was in place.

"May have?"

"He's got a reputation for not taking no for an answer. A month after he made her his private secretary, she left his employ verra suddenly, with nary a reference. She had a bit of difficulty securing another position. A woman named Laura Roswell finally gave her a job."

"Is all of this relevant?"

"I think so. She's not married. She's not involved with anyone. In fact, she's hardly had any social life in the past few years—except with her women friends at the Light Street address. And Marconi was her last living relative." He paused for a moment.

"What aren't you telling me?"

"Nothing. I just wasn't able to get much information on her before she came to work for Gilmore."

"I could do some poking around the old neighborhood, if you like. People might tell me things they wouldn't confide to an outsider."

"No, that's not necessary. I have what I need. Now that Marconi's dead, I may press her into service."

"There's a big risk in using an untrained courier."

"Of course. But in this case, it won't matter. She's completely expendable. The Emery lass vanishes, and no one wastes a lot of time looking for her. What do you think?''

Jason inclined his head slightly. ''I think you've got a diabolically clever mind.''

''Yes, well, I only make the plans. You're the one who's going to dispose of her if the need arises.''

Chapter Three

Noel stopped outside the stream of pedestrian traffic converging on the security barrier at Baltimore-Washington International Airport. Rifling thorough her purse, she found the travel agency envelope with her ticket. "This is as far as you can go," she said to Abby.

"It's not too late to change your mind."

"I think this is the right decision." She smiled reassuringly, conscious of how much effort it was taking for her to appear absolutely in control. But she wasn't going to give Abby any reason to doubt her stability.

"I'd be happier if you were staying home," Abby murmured.

"I may be too scatterbrained to work, but I can still deliver a boxful of jewelry to Flora Marconi."

"You're *not* scatterbrained. You just need to stop pushing yourself."

"That's what I have in mind. A vacation."

Abby nodded. "Well, this *is* a lovely time of year to be in England. There are spring flowers all over the place, and it's lambing season. As soon as you've met with your uncle's ex-wife, find yourself a nice little village where there's nothing to do but relax and watch the lambs play."

Noel smiled. It was about time her friend gave up trying to change her mind. They'd been over the pros and cons of the trip a dozen times, and Noel had been steadfast in her resolve to accommodate Flora Marconi. On some deep level of consciousness, it was as if she didn't have any choice about the trip. As if she had to go, come hell or high water.

"Honey, if you need anything at all—or if you just want to talk—call me collect."

"Stop worrying about me."

The two friends hugged goodbye. Then Noel rejoined the line of departing passengers. When her turn came, she hoisted her bag onto the moving belt for the X-ray machine and stepped through the metal detector.

On the other side of the barrier, she waited for her luggage.

"Is this yours?" the guard asked, pointing to the navy-blue-and-red carryall.

"Yes."

"Please open it for inspection."

Noel felt her tension grow as the security guard searched carefully through the contents and finally brought out the velvet padded box of jewelry she was bringing to Flora Marconi.

She hadn't even known Uncle Henry had been married until a woman with an upper-class British accent had called and started crying over the phone. When she'd gotten better control of herself, she'd given Noel a long-distance account of her whole life history. Apparently Henry and Flora had met when he'd been on assignment with the army in England. She'd tried life in the States, Flora had explained with a little sniff of distaste, but she'd realized she just wasn't happy living away from her people. Although she'd gone back home, she and Henry had continued to see each other on his frequent trips to Britain. She was shocked to the core by his death, which she'd learned about so coldly when she'd been notified by his lawyer about his will.

She'd been told Henry's jewelry was already in Noel's name. But there were a few pieces that Flora hoped she could acquire because they were of great sentimental value. Would his niece be a dear and bring them over to London? Flora would pay for the baubles and the trip— because she longed to meet the niece Henry had loved almost as much as a daughter.

In her present state, Noel had been grateful for a chance to stop feeling useless. Luckily, since she lived so close to Washington, D.C., she was able to expedite her passport application through the State Department.

"Would you unlock this?" The guard extended the jewel box to Noel.

Unable to understand why she felt so nervous, she held her breath as he poked through the contents and lifted out an enormous, starburst-shaped brooch set with a topaz about the size of a nickel.

"Is everything all right?"

He turned the piece over in his hand. "I'd like to see the interior of this."

"What are you looking for?"

"Just open it up, please."

Noel complied and was relieved to see that a packet of white powder or something equally incriminating had not materialized inside the compartment in the center of the brooch.

The man snapped the cover shut and put the starburst back into the box.

"Thank you for your cooperation."

Noel collected her things and hurried down the pier toward the departure lounge. What could you put in a piece of jewelry that would compromise security?

One moment she was thinking about the brooch. In the next, she was unable to think at all. Just before she reached the waiting area, her brain went muzzy.

Chaos

Missing her footing, she would have ended up on the carpet, except that a short, balding man in a tweed sports coat caught her arm.

"Are you all right, Miss?"

"Yes," she managed. "Thanks." Standing very still, Noel sucked in a deep breath. Then, with every ounce of concentration she could muster, she focused on putting one foot in front of the other as she made her way through the doorway toward one of the bucket seats along the wall.

Eyes squeezed tight, she sat with her chin in her hands, waiting for the attack to go away. She'd thought—no, she'd hoped—but here it was again.

Damn. She hated this. Hated the feeling of . . . chaos.

She'd be okay for hours. A whole day, even. Physically and mentally. She'd tell herself she was finally getting better. Then—slam-bang—it was as if someone had switched on a high-powered broadcast signal and her mind was a satellite receiver.

Noel grimaced. It wasn't a broadcast exactly. There was only one distinguishable word that jumped out of the background noise when the attacks were at their worst.

Chaos

Sometimes she caught the vague suggestion of images. But mostly there was simply the crackling of static. Static that flickered along her brain synapses like the flickering and bursts of sound from a TV set when the station wasn't quite tuned in. Static that made it almost impossible to think.

Noel had been too frightened to describe the sensation to Abby. She didn't want to hear a scary diagnosis. But that hadn't prevented her from sneaking into her friend's study and thumbing through a bunch of medical books. Her throat had clogged when she'd come to the material on seizures.

According to the literature, abnormal brain wave patterns and epileptic episodes could be precipitated in a heretofore normal individual by a blow to the head.

However, the symptoms described in the medical texts weren't quite what she was experiencing. She wasn't having grand mal seizures. At least, nobody had found her unconscious and twitching on the floor. And she couldn't call these episodes petit mal, either. That was where you went into a sort of trance and snapped out of it in a few seconds.

As far as she could tell, the books didn't cover anything like what was happening to her. Which might be reassuring—if she wanted to believe she was doing this to herself. Maybe it *would* all go away if she could hole up in some English country village and relax.

Sitting perfectly still, she silently willed the attack to subside. One thing was becoming all too clear: stress was part of the problem. If she could only get herself to relax, she'd feel better.

Gradually the strategy worked, and she sighed with relief. All she needed was to get away. Still, if she didn't feel better by the time she got home, she could go back to the doctor. The man in the tweed jacket kept glancing across the aisle at her. Sitting up straighter, Noel smiled at him and tried to look as if she were just fine.

Twenty minutes later, the flight began to board.

THE MAN TRAVELING on a passport that named him as Frank Jackson, owner of a small printing business in Randallstown, Maryland, waited inconspicuously outside the departure lounge until Noel disappeared down the jetway. Then he, too, boarded, taking his seat eighteen rows behind her on the double-aisled plane. He'd planned the seating arrangement so that he wouldn't be too close but could still keep an eye on her during the flight.

After a few noncommittal responses, he managed to discourage any further attempts at conversation on the part of the couple next to him. Instead he bought the earphones the flight attendant offered and pretended to be engrossed in the music program. Sounds from the sixties. The Beatles, The Who, and the Rolling Stones. Funny how the cutting edge in pop music faded to nostalgia.

Not that he was really paying attention to the music. He could see only the top of Noel's head, but he felt her presence like the heat from a forest fire.

How would she react to him? With a wry grimace, Jason answered his own question: she wouldn't. Because Frank Jackson resembled Jason Zacharias about as much as a sloppy joe did a gyro sandwich. A heavy disguise on a seven-hour transatlantic flight was a drag, so he'd kept things simple. Contact lenses to lighten his eyes, heavily rimmed glasses, and lightweight padding around his waist and across his chest to give the appearance of twenty extra pounds. The somewhat sloppy effect was enhanced by the way he'd combed his hair and by the shambling gait he affected when he walked—and at present, by his low slouch in the seat.

Outwardly he looked relaxed. Inwardly he'd given up trying to untie the knots clenching his stomach.

He'd spent the past few years conjuring up scenarios and making contingency plans, and they hadn't included lying to the Sovereign about his background or his day-to-day handling of assignments. It was too risky. The man was too good a judge of motives.

It had been bad enough when he'd only been gambling with his own life. Now the stakes had doubled.

He silently cursed the ancient Greek goddesses of fate, who were probably having a good laugh at his expense right now. In the past few months, he'd told himself he was prepared for anything. Then Noel had walked into the middle of the most dangerous game of his checkered career.

He closed his eyes, picturing her sitting innocent and unaware in the rows ahead of him. He'd known the first time he'd taken her out all those years ago how easy it would be to get her into trouble.

The memory of their first kiss came rushing back to him, as sharp and sweet and dangerous as ever. Smooth-talking Jason Zacharias had started out to seduce naive little Noel Emery. But when he wrapped his arms around her and covered her soft lips with his, the balance of power had shifted subtly. She made his knees week and his hands tremble.

Back then he'd told himself he was doing Noel Emery a favor by running away from her. He'd even convinced himself that he didn't need—didn't want—a nice girl like her. After the passion wore off, she'd be boring. And she'd try to make him shape up. Marry her. Get a job so he could support a family.

He'd done a lot of running away since he'd skipped his senior year of high school and enlisted in the marines. But fate had a strange way of weaving you back into the pattern you'd tried to escape.

A shudder careened through his body. What if he had to make a choice? His life or hers? The success of the operation or her life?

"Are you all right?" The voice of the woman next to him filtered though his distress.

With a curt nod he got up and made his way to the bathrooms. He longed to splash cold water on his face, but it would mess up the makeup that lightened his skin color. Instead he stood with his head bowed and his hands rigid on the metal sink, trying to think himself out of this mess. He struggled for the necessary mental discipline, but it eluded him. Deep in his soul he knew the only way he could avoid the awful trade-offs was if he was very lucky—and if he played things exactly right.

JASON FORCED HIMSELF to eat some of the reheated chicken dinner. By the time the flight attendants turned down the lights for the feature video presentation, he was feeling strangely calm. In the dim light, he stood up, stretched and glanced at Noel. Like most of the passengers, she was watching the movie, and he knew from previewing the flick that an engrossing sequence was coming up.

Ambling up the aisle toward the back of the aircraft, he waited his turn, then stepped into one of the toilet compartments. After locking the door, he got out the tiny transmitter he was carrying and held it up in front of the mirror. The casing looked like an extra button for the raincoat Noel had purchased for the trip. It was timed to activate after the plane landed.

When he stepped into the aisle again, the miniature gadget was in the palm of his hand. Instead of heading directly back to his row, Jason made his way slowly up the other side of the plane, halting as he neared Noel's seat. As he'd hoped, she appeared to be absorbed in the movie. In addition, the flight had hit a bit of rough air, which was also to his advantage. As he drew even with the passengers in back of Noel, the seat belt sign flashed on. All he had to do was wait for another lurch of the cabin. Then he pretended to stumble, dropping his glasses case in the process.

"Damn," he murmured, kneeling down on the floor beside the seats. When the woman to his right glanced in his direction, he smiled sheepishly and pointed toward the case.

Waiting until she'd returned her attention to the action on the screen, Jason pushed the eyeglass case farther along the floor until it was next to Noel's leather pocketbook. As he retrieved his property, he slid the button deep into the side pocket of the purse. He was betting she wouldn't even find it. If she did, she'd probably assume it was an extra from the raincoat that had somehow gotten misplaced.

At SIX IN THE MORNING, one hundred and sixty travel-weary passengers exited down the jetway at Gatwick, collected their luggage and piled it onto the carts provided. As they took the moving sidewalk from the satellite terminal to the brightly lit immigration-and-customs processing area, Jason stayed well behind Noel.

She was wearing black slacks and a long-sleeved, jade green cotton shirt, so it wasn't difficult to keep her in sight.

He was about ten minutes from having his passport inspected when he sensed that something was wrong. Most of the passengers were being checked through after a few routine questions about their reasons for visiting the British Isles and the length of their stay. But the blue-uniformed woman interviewing Noel was taking longer. As he watched with growing concern, she motioned to a supervisor.

The expression on Noel's face told him that she was worried. His own mouth suddenly dry, Jason edged forward, trying to hear the exchange. When the man in front of him turned and scowled, he sighed and stepped back into line.

There was nothing he could do but wait and hope for the best. But he wasn't surprised when another official appeared and the two of them escorted Noel off toward a doorway on the other side of the barrier.

THE ROOM WAS SMALL and cold and smelled vaguely of disinfectant. Like the rest of the intake area, it was also brightly lit. There was nothing welcoming or cheerful, however, about the harsh fluorescent glow.

Noel guessed that the guard who closed the door and seated her in a metal chair was about her age. She didn't like the way he moved back toward the door so she couldn't bolt.

Another man who looked to be in his fifties was sitting behind a desk. He had gray hair, a neatly trimmed mustache, and a military bearing that made Noel think of a character actor playing the part of a distinguished British colonel. The name tag on his uniform jacket said Welby. She'd already noted that the younger one was called Fenton.

Noel clenched her fingers in her lap while Welby looked through some papers on the desk and the passport that had been taken away from her. She watched his hands and his eyes while she pressed her back against the vertical slats of the metal chair.

If only her brain were working better. But the combination of jet lag and the recent concussion made her head feel as if it were oozing molasses instead of processing thoughts.

Why was she being singled out again? It was as if she were wearing some kind of sign on her back that read I'm Planning To Bomb Number 10 Downing Street.

Blood pounded in Noel's ears as she waited for Welby to speak. Finally the silence became intolerable. "You can't just hold me here without any explanation," she blurted.

"We simply want to clear up a few points. Miss Noel Emery, is it?"

"Yes."

A polite enough beginning, but then, the British were notoriously polite.

"Isn't my passport in order?"

He opened the navy blue booklet once again, looked at Noel's picture and ran his thumb over the raised seal. Then he asked where she lived, and she gave the address he could see very well for himself.

"Thank you very much."

They went back through the questions she'd already answered in the immigration hall.

"This passport was issued only two days ago. It's quite unusual to be traveling on such a recent document."

"That's not illegal."

"Quite so."

The silence lengthened again, and she felt compelled to explain further. "I only decided to make this trip at the beginning of the week, so I went down to the State Department and had things expedited."

"This is emergency travel, then?"

"No, not an emergency. I was asked to do a favor for my uncle's widow."

"Would you mind giving us the details?"

Noel skipped the robbery and started with the simple fact of her uncle's death, Flora Marconi's notification about the will, and her subsequent call. Digging into her purse, she got out the address Flora had given her. "I'm supposed to meet her as soon as I get into London. Or call if there are any problems." She handed him a copy of the information she'd been given.

"Well, that's simple enough to verify. We'll get this cleared up straight away." Welby gave the paper to Fenton, who opened the door and passed it to someone in the hall.

My God, Noel thought, the other guard was still lurking outside. But really, she assured herself, there was nothing to worry about. Welby was right: the facts were easily verifiable. She'd be out of here and on her way in a couple of minutes.

Fenton was gone longer than she'd expected. Instead of sitting and staring at the man on the other side of the desk, she dug out the paperback novel she'd brought along and tried to concentrate on the words. They swam in front of her eyes, and it didn't help knowing that Welby was sitting across the desk watching her. Still she kept her head bent, grimly staring at the print.

When the door opened again, they both looked up expectantly.

"That address is for a furnished town house in South Kensington."

Yes, that was where Flora had said she lived.

"The previous tenant moved out last week, and the property is still to let." Fenton delivered the message impassively, but the words brought a sick feeling to the pit of Noel's stomach.

With fingers that had turned clammy, she accepted the paper again and scanned the address. "Are you sure you have the right house? There must be some mistake."

"No mistake, miss. I verified the address through the computer system at the Central London Estate Agent registry. When the property came up unoccupied, I rang up the city police department and requested a visual check. They had a car in the area and were able to report back immediately."

Noel swallowed around the lump that had materialized in her throat. "Did you check the phone number?" she asked.

"Certainly. When I identified myself, the woman who answered hung up."

"We can ring up again from here," Welby offered helpfully.

"Yes." With shaky fingers, Noel tried to follow his dialing instructions. It took two tries before she got anything to happen. Then she didn't know how to interpret the double sets of honking noises. "Is it ringing?" she asked, handing the phone to Welby. "Or is that a busy signal?"

He listened. "It's ringing."

She waited tensely through ten or fifteen repetitions.

"Well, it does seem as if we have a problem," Welby said as she gave up and put down the phone.

Noel couldn't meet his eyes. She had a problem, all right. But why? What was going on?

"I think you'd better give us a full account of your contact with this Flora Marconi," Welby said.

"It's just what I told you."

"You might explain why you neglected to mention that your uncle was shot to death."

Noel gulped. "You know about that?"

Welby nodded.

"I see. Is that why you hauled me in here in the first place? What does customs have to do with a Baltimore murder?"

"We received a tip linking an American traveling under the name of Noel Emery from Baltimore to London with an international smuggling operation. That triggered a check of your recent activities."

"Smuggling! That's ridiculous."

"Is it?"

"Check my luggage."

"We intend to. Every inch of it. And your person, as well."

A strip search? Noel cringed. To mask her alarm, she drew herself up straighter. "I am an American citizen. You can't do this to me." But even as the protest tumbled from her lips, she realized the weakness of her position. Last year she'd taken a course in international law. When an American citizen got into trouble overseas, she was subject to the laws and regulations of the host country. The only lucky thing was that she wasn't facing some power-drunk Third World functionary who'd throw her in a cell and keep her whereabouts to himself while he gleefully contemplated bribery and ransom.

"We have probable cause to detain you," Welby said in the calmly rational voice that was driving her crazy.

"I want to speak to the American embassy."

"After the search. Perhaps we'll find nothing, and you can continue with your holiday—no harm done." His tone of voice didn't support the conclusion.

"Perhaps I'll sue you for false arrest," Noel shot back, the defiance in her voice belying the sick feeling in her midsection.

"This isn't an arrest. No charges have been filed. You're simply being detained for questioning. We'll know soon enough whether anything more is in order."

"Wait. You say you're acting on a tip. Where did it come from?"

"We're not at liberty to divulge that information," Welby said.

Fenton moved in closer behind Noel as if he expected her to run.

The older man stood up. "Come along, then, miss."

"Where . . . where are you taking me?" Noel couldn't keep her voice from rising in panic at the end of the question.

"To another facility."

"But—you can't—" Noel stopped abruptly, knowing that if she tried to say anything else, she'd break down. And she was determined to hold on to that much of her dignity.

Welby draped Noel's coat over her shoulders. When Fenton opened the door, she saw her luggage piled in the hall. The same red-and-blue bag that had given her problems at BWI. And the almost-matching suitcase that she'd borrowed from Abby. She stared at the bags. Was it just a coincidence that she'd been stopped at the start of the trip, too? Or had some sort of warning been issued about her in Baltimore, as well? If that was true, why had they let her leave?

Then an even more sinister thought struck her. What if "Flora" had set her up? But why?

"It will be better for you if you cooperate," Welby said.

"There's nothing more I can tell you."

Fenton kept a firm grip on her arm. The other man picked up the luggage. The mismatched quartet took a side door that opened onto a parking area for official vehicles.

The sky was overcast, and rain spattered on the blacktop. Fenton hurried Noel along to a small blue Vauxhall and ushered her into the back seat. There was a mesh barrier between the front and back of the car. The lock clicked as Fenton closed the door and went to stow the luggage in the back. Noel stared at the driver, momentarily confused that he was on the wrong side of the car.

Fenton joined them, and they backed out of the parking place. Noel cringed against the cold plastic seat and watched the rain-streaked airport buildings slide past. This wasn't happening. It couldn't be happening.

But it was.

They merged with a stream of exit traffic onto a six-lane highway. It could have been the Baltimore beltway at morning rush hour, except that the vehicles were moving in the wrong direction.

After several miles, they turned onto a secondary road to somewhere called East Grinstead. The lanes were narrow by American standards, and the scenery became more and more rural. For long stretches there was nothing but green fields full of grazing sheep. Noel had assumed her jailers were taking her into the city. Instead, they were heading toward the middle of nowhere. Why?

About a mile past a little village, Noel heard a loud popping sound. Almost at once, the car began to sway. Cursing, the driver slowed and maneuvered toward the shoulder.

"Blowout?" Fenton asked, giving Noel a quick look before turning his attention back to the driver.

"'Fraid so." The man brought the car to a bouncing halt, making Noel suddenly dizzy. She closed her eyes and gripped the hand rest.

"I'll have a look, then."

Noel opened her eyes again to see Fenton had unstrapped his seat belt. He was reaching for the door handle when a large white vehicle with a flashing light on top pulled up behind them.

"Hold on a bit, mate. Looks as if we're in luck. A service lorry's stopping."

As a compact but muscular man wearing gray overalls and a visor cap approached the car, the driver rolled down the window. "Glad you were behind us."

"'Avin' a spot o' trouble, I see." The newcomer leaned his balding head toward the window.

"Blowout."

"Well, I'm just the chap to put things right." A large hand came up toward the driver's neck. There was a hissing noise, and the man slumped forward over the steering wheel.

Noel screamed and shrank back against the seat.

Fenton grabbed frantically at the door handle. But he never got out of the car. Another hiss, and he joined his companion. Then the hand shifted toward Noel, and all she could see was an ugly little pistol flattened against the palm.

Chapter Four

Noel stared uncomprehendingly as the man's hard expression evaporated.

"Just in the nick of time! Did those bloody coppers mess you about?" he asked.

She gaped at him.

"Come on, love. We're getting outa here while the gettin's good."

Still she shrank away. "You shot them."

"They're just grabbing a snooze." The lorry driver held up his little weapon. "Tranquilizer gun."

Noel tried to make sense of what was happening. A few moments ago she'd been in the custody of the customs service. Now her guards were out cold. "You—you're rescuing me?"

"Right. I'm here to make sure nothing happens to you." As he spoke, he unlocked the back door of the car.

When Noel hesitated, he gestured impatiently. "Come on, then."

Noel didn't want to get any closer to him. But she hadn't liked being hustled away from the airport, either, or being locked in the back of the car. Stepping out on the shoulder of the road, she steadied herself with a hand against the door and looked uncertainly from her rescuer to his truck. "Why are you doing this? How do you even know who I am?"

"Well, love, we had a man at customs lookin' out for you. He got on the horn as soon as they took you out of the building."

"Why?" she repeated.

He smiled disarmingly. "The stuffed shirts are a bit dim when it comes to what you can bring into the country. But my employer has a proposition that could make you a very wealthy woman, if you'll just give us a few hours of your time."

"Your employer? Who is that?"

"Mr. Montgomery. He's very anxious to meet you and have a look at the information you're carrying."

"Information I'm carrying?"

"You're a cagey one, you are."

Noel's head was spinning. "The man you work for arranges to have customs agents tranquilized?"

"Better than arguing with them over a technicality."

"But—"

"I can answer your questions on the road. Let me get your kit from the boot." Reaching inside the car, he pulled the key from the ignition. Then he sauntered around to the rear, opened the trunk and took out Noel's luggage.

In growing alarm, Noel scanned the rolling green countryside and the stretch of road. In the far distance was a vehicle, and she could see a church spire. But the only living things in the immediate vicinity were a straggly flock of black-faced sheep. At least the customs service would have a record of her being detained and taken away. If she went off with this man, she could disappear without a trace.

Noel swallowed, feeling as if she'd stepped from real life into a James Bond film. She remembered what happened to so many of the women in those movies. They ended up dead.

"Wait a minute. I haven't agreed to anything," she protested. "Who is this Mr. Montgomery? And what's his business?"

"I told you, I'll explain on the way." He was beginning to sound impatient. "Come on. Before somebody figures out you've gone missing."

What if she refused to go along with his plans?

The truck driver set the luggage on the ground. When he leaned over to unlock the rear door of his vehicle, she saw an oddly shaped implement sticking out of one of his coverall pockets. It had a leather shaft and a bulbous end like a microphone. A blackjack. She remembered it from when a battered wife had brought one into Laura's office. It wasn't the kind of hardware an honest man carried.

Looking wildly around for a weapon of her own, she snatched up the red-and-blue carryall by the handle, stepped back to give herself more room, and swung the heavy bag as hard as she could. When she let it fly, it smacked the truck driver hard in the back of the neck, and he pitched forward through the open doors of the lorry.

Turning, she sprinted toward the low stone wall that bounded the closest pasture. She hadn't been very active since she'd gotten out of the hospital, and in moments, she was panting and her chest felt as if it were on fire. An angry string of curses behind her sent her hurtling over the wall.

Black-faced sheep and lambs scattered, bleating anxiously, as Noel came down, her feet sinking into the damp grass. Blood was roaring in her ears, but she forced herself to keep moving.

Behind her, she heard the screech of brakes. The motorist was stopping to find out what had happened, which might give her more time. She didn't think about what she was going to do if she got away. She just ran, her breath coming in knife-sharp gasps, her shoes caked with mud and her side aching.

"Noel, stop!"

She faltered for a moment. The voice sounded American, not like the truck driver. But who knew what accent was his real one?

She didn't dare risk a glance behind her. As she broke through a little grove of trees, she heard someone crashing through the underbrush, gaining on her. She turned and raced for another stone wall a few hundred feet away. Even as she ran, she could feel the remains of her strength ebbing away and a drumming dizziness seeping into her brain.

Chaos

Oh, no. No! It was happening again.

But she wouldn't let it get her. She wouldn't!

Gritting her teeth, she forced her mind to focus and her legs to keep working. The stone wall shimmered before her like a mirage in the desert. She was almost there. Just a few more steps. She could make it. With every ounce of determination she possessed, she lunged forward. Her hands connected with hard stone, and she vaulted over the ledge. Her legs flexed as she anticipated another level field. Instead her feet came down on loose stones at the verge of a hill that dropped to a basin below. There was no way to stop her forward momentum. With a scream, she felt herself toppling over the edge.

She hit the bottom with a dull thud and lay motionless, gasping for breath. After a few moments, it registered that she had landed on a pile of leaves and hay that had cushioned her fall.

Pushing herself to her feet, she stood swaying.

"Noel!"

In the next moment, a large male figure was crashing down the side of the hill. Quickly. Recklessly.

Panic rising in her throat, she tried to run. Before she took more than a few shaky steps, large hands clamped down on her shoulders.

A gasp tore from her lips.

Caught. After all that.

"Sweetheart, I'm not going to hurt you."

She tried to twist away, pounding at his hands and then at his broad chest and shoulders as he turned her around.

"Noel. Stop. It's all right. It's Jason."

The familiar timbre and rhythm of his voice, as much as the urgent grip of his large hands on her arms, gentled her. Yet she was still dazed and unable to process what was happening.

She forgot to breathe as she stared at him, her fingers clenching the gray sweater that covered his torso, her eyes searching his face.

It had been so long. . . .

Or had it?

"Jason?"

"Yes."

Amazement expanded inside her chest. She couldn't believe the evidence of her senses. Her fingers twisted deeper into the fabric, desperate to hold him there. With her. "Is it really you?"

"It's really me."

"How . . . ?"

"I came to help you."

She still didn't understand, but she clutched at his words, just as she held tight to his solid form. He had come to help her before. Long ago...and...again a wisp of memory fluttered tantalizingly through her brain. Like a child chasing a butterfly, she tried to catch it, but it was gone before she could close her thoughts around more than shimmering gossamer.

"Are you all right?"

Noel blinked and tried to form an answer. "I—yes."

The world had contracted to his tousled dark hair, his achingly familiar features, his ebony eyes boring down into her blue ones.

Suddenly the reality of finding Jason Zacharias here, now, was too much. Her knees buckled and he caught her, holding her tightly against his solid body, his hand coming up to twine in her hair and stroke the back of her neck.

She closed her eyes, wanting to shut out everything but Jason. It felt so good to be in his arms again. The only place where she'd ever been safe. Or perhaps there was no such place. She inhaled his familiar scent, ran her hands over his shoulders and down his arms, feeling the corded muscles flex under her fingers. She raised her head again, her eyes begging him to answer a question she didn't know how to phrase.

"Are you sure you're all right?" he asked again.

"I am now." As she said the words, she felt a profound sense of well-being settle over her. And a rush of need that went far beyond anything merely physical.

She saw his eyes darken, his expression waver between something soft and something primitive that made her heart turn over.

"Noel. Ah, God, Noel." His mouth touched hers, and he murmured the words indistinctly against her lips, as if coherence was less important than maintaining the contact.

With a little sigh, she opened to him, welcomed him.

"I tried—I can't—" Until that moment, his kiss had been gentle. Suddenly it turned deep and urgent as if all earthly needs had coalesced into this one powerful contact with each other.

He tasted, probed, demanded a response from her that would have been impossible to express in words. Yet she could give it to him with her body, with her very soul.

She kissed him back with the same reckless fervor, her lips moving wildly against his, her fingers winnowing through his thick, ebony hair.

The tender, yearning part of her had been crusted over with ice. But the long, dark winter was over. This man had brought with him the age-old magic of sunshine, pouring down upon the cold earth, stirring life anew.

When he dragged his mouth away from hers, she whimpered. She wanted it to go on. If he simply kept holding her in his arms, kissing her, touching her, she wouldn't have to think. She would only have to feel.

But as she stared up into the fierce urgency of his eyes, she knew he wasn't going to give her that comfort. "When was the last time you saw me?"

She tried to make sense of the question. "Don't you know?"

"Yes. But I want you to tell me."

"In...in...Mr. Dubinski's shop."

She saw the spark die in his eyes. "You don't remember."

"Remember what?" Her hands tightened on his arms, as she tried to force herself to think. But her mind had stopped functioning in the old, familiar patterns weeks ago.

He shook his head. "It doesn't matter."

"Tell me."

"Later."

The disappointment on his face tore at her insides.

"What are we to each other?" she whispered.

For just a moment, pain filled his eyes. "You have to find that out for yourself."

"Help me."

"I can't. Not now." His lips were set in a grim line. She studied his features, taking in details she'd missed. With a trembling finger, she touched a faded scar over his left cheekbone.

The last time she'd seen him had been in a room where the light wasn't so bright. Where she hadn't been able to get a good look at him. Or maybe her vision had been blurred.

The last time? What kind of tricks was her mind playing? The last time was . . .

He stood very still as he gazed down into her eyes.

"What happened to you?" she whispered, gently tracing the scar.

He swallowed. "An explosion."

"Were you badly hurt?"

"I survived."

She was trembling at the brink of knowledge that was desperately important. "Tell me—"

"Noel, we can't stay here. We have to clear out before somebody finds the men in the car."

Fenton and the driver. She'd forgotten all about them—about everything but Jason.

"Noel, we can't stand here talking."

"We weren't just talking."

His gaze went to her lips. For a moment ripe with anticipation, she thought he might take her in his arms again. But it didn't happen; instead, he tugged gently at her hand.

Noel didn't move. Closing her eyes, she took a deep breath, trying to clear her thoughts. Was it all a dream? A man from her past. Appearing from nowhere and chasing her across the English countryside. Pulling her against the hard length of his body and kissing her. Awakening a longing deep inside her being. She squeezed her fingers around his. Flesh and blood and bone. Yes. He was real. But anchoring herself to warm flesh didn't help. In fact, it made things worse.

"Come on."

She couldn't cope with her feelings. She couldn't even think coherently. With a little sigh, she gave in to the longing to let him take charge. Now that he was here, he would make everything come out right.

When he slipped an arm over her shoulders, she settled against him and let him lead her back across the field. This time they took a different route to avoid the hill she'd tumbled down.

Yet even as he steered her back to the road, Noel kept glancing at the man beside her, trying to remember... something. His face was an unreadable mask, as if he'd said too much and was determined not to give anything more. But he'd said nothing. Nothing that she needed to hear. Somehow, that helped strip off a few of the dreamlike layers that wrapped her mind.

"The truck driver. What happened to the truck driver?"

"I took care of him."

She blinked, concentrating her mind and forcing her awareness to another level. My God, she was so out of it that she hadn't even asked the most obvious question. "What are you doing here?"

"I'm going to make sure nothing happens to you."

"*He* said that, too. When he tried to get me to go with him."

Another expression she couldn't read flickered across Jason's face. She should be getting used to that, but she didn't like it.

"Are you really here to help me?" she asked.

"You have to trust me."

"I used to."

He was silent for several moments. "How did you get away?"

"From the man? I hit him with my flight bag and ran."

"Good girl."

They had come up within sight of the road. Three vehicles were lined up, the car with the customs agents inside, the truck, and another smaller sedan. Jason's.

As Noel stared at them, the most logical question of all tumbled from her lips. "How did you know where to find me?"

"I followed you from the airport."

"How?"

"There's a transmitter in your purse."

She turned and stared at him. "What are you talking about?"

"It's a little device that broadcasts a signal. It's got a directional finder. The closer you get, the stronger the signal. The receiver is in my car."

It was a strange conversation, because part of her mind had no trouble following his matter-of-fact explanation. But she felt like Alice in Wonderland listening to the Red Queen. "Are you going to tell me what's going on?"

"As much as I can."

"You came to get me away from the man who was trying to kidnap me from the authorities."

"That's as good an explanation as any."

As they drew abreast of the first car, Noel glanced inside. Fenton and the driver were still slumped in the front seat.

"The longer lead time we have, the better," Jason said as he took her elbow and hurried her toward the truck. When he opened the back door, Noel peered inside, seeing a pair of feet and legs clad in gray overalls.

"Give me a minute." Jason disappeared into the interior, closing the door.

Noel looked from the van to Jason's car. Until now, she'd been under a kind of spell, docilely going along with his plans. With an incredulous shake of her head, she wondered precisely what was wrong with her. Was it just the head injury making her act this way? Or was it something more? As she looked nervously up and down the road, a motorist slowed and stared at her. She stifled the impulse to run toward him, waving. What would she say if he stopped? The moment passed and the car disappeared over the crest of a hill—leaving Noel with the notion that Jason was just as dangerous as the man in the truck.

Her heart began to thump as she thought about making a run for it again. Then she shook her head, trying to rid herself of the half-formed idea. She was banged up and exhausted. How far could she get, even if she tried?

More than that, deep inside, she desperately wanted to believe that she could trust Jason Zacharias.

The door opened. Jason got out and handed Noel her purse. Then he retrieved her luggage. All of which she'd forgotten.

She was about to issue automatic thanks, when he reached inside to pull out some additional items. He turned back to Noel, and her eyes bugged out as she saw he was holding an ugly-looking machine gun.

"Your friend had more than that toy pistol with him."

"What are you going to do with them?"

"They might come in handy."

In what kind of situation? she wondered as he slammed the door. Then he was ushering her toward the car.

When he opened the door, she stiffened her arm against the frame. Her heart was thumping, and it was all she could do to stop herself from bolting. "Where are we going?"

"A safe place."

She turned and looked up, pleading, into his eyes.

He swallowed. "Are you afraid of me?"

"I don't want to be."

"Noel, I'd never hurt you." He pulled her to him, brushing his lips against her cheek.

"Oh, Jason. It's all so…frightening. And unreal." She wished she could tell him how confused she felt. Or was that exactly the wrong thing to do?

"Let me take care of everything. For now."

In her present state, she wanted more than life itself to believe he was on her side. And, really, what choice did she have?

With a tight nod, she climbed into the car.

Jason stowed the weapons in the truck, started the engine and nosed the car onto the blacktop. At first he headed in the direction they'd all been traveling from the airport. Before he reached East Grinstead, he turned onto an ever-narrowing track. Noel watched him shift gears. They were in the middle of the English countryside, but he seemed to know exactly where he was going. He also seemed completely comfortable driving on the wrong side of the road and shifting with the wrong hand.

The route took them past open fields, farms and villages of stone cottages with carefully tended flower gardens. Sometimes there were pubs identified by signs colorfully painted with illustrations and names like The White Swan or The Stag.

Jason hadn't said a word since they'd gotten into the car.

"Tell me why I shouldn't run screaming to the nearest police station," she finally blurted.

Jason took his eyes from the road for a moment and studied her. "That wouldn't be very smart," he said in a tone that he hadn't used before.

"Why?"

"Because you're a fugitive from the British authorities, and someone else is after you, as well."

"Who?"

This time, Jason didn't glance away from the road. "Whoever the guy with the stun gun is working for."

"Montgomery?"

Jason's brows lifted.

"You know him?" she asked.

"Not personally."

"The truck driver said he wants to make me a rich woman."

"I wouldn't count on it."

She wanted answers. Jason's clipped replies gave away very little. And the molasses feeling in her head made it hard to summon up the energy to frame more questions. But the doubts she'd tried to shove from her mind were gnawing at her again.

With a grimace, Noel struggled for mental coherence. Jason was a puzzle she didn't know how to solve. But what about the rest? First there was Flora—who wasn't at the address or phone number she'd given Noel. Was she part of a conspiracy? Or had the people working for Mr. Montgomery picked up Henry's ex-wife, too?

A conspiracy. On the face of it, the idea was ridiculous. Who would mount a conspiracy against a Baltimore paralegal on vacation in Britain? But then why did the customs service think she was a smuggler?

From under lowered lashes she studied Jason. She hadn't seen him for years. He looked a world removed from the lanky teenage rebel who had taken her out a few times and then dropped her. Yet back in the meadow she'd had no trouble recognizing him as soon as she'd calmed down enough to realize who was grasping her shoulders. In fact, she'd felt a startling rush of warm, tender emotions for a man who had once made it very clear that the two of them had nothing to give each other.

"When *was* the last time I saw you?" she asked suddenly.

"After your uncle died."

Before she could assimilate that information, he was asking a question of his own. "What do you remember about the shooting in the jewelry shop?"

"Nothing. I was in the back room putting rings away. The next thing I knew I was waking up in the hospital. Some stranger took me there." As she said the words, a shiver rippled over her skin. "You. It was you."

"Yes. How have you been since then?"

"Okay. If you discount the amnesia and the dizzy spells."

His head snapped toward her and then back to the road. "Dizzy spells? You mean you're still having symptoms?"

"My physician tells me they'll go away." She looked at his stony profile. It helped focus her attention. "We were talking about you. How did you happen to come into the shop?"

"I was in the vicinity."

"Are you in Baltimore often?"

"Not often."

The image that had come to her when she'd been talking to Abby that afternoon in the garden fluttered back. "What are you, some kind of guardian angel who swoops down to help every time I'm in trouble?"

He snorted. "Hardly."

"Then what—?"

"Noel, I'm sorry. But the more you know about what's going on, the more dangerous it is."

"That's crazy."

"I said you're just going to have to trust me."

She didn't. Couldn't. Not when he'd raised more doubts than he'd answered. Just then, they turned off the road onto a private lane hemmed in by tall hedges. She looked up at the wall of greenery, feeling as if all hope of escape had suddenly been cut off. But that was ridiculous. He wasn't taking her to an armed fortress, was he?

The car swung around a corner. Noel felt a surge of relief when they pulled into a gravel parking area in front of a stone cottage that looked as if it could have illustrated the cover of a book on British country life. The thatched roof was steeply sloped. The windows had small, diamond-shaped panes, and a vine with tiny purple flowers twined up the wall and across the top of the door.

"Who lives here?" Noel asked as Jason opened the driver's door.

"Us. For the moment."

He retrieved her luggage from the back, along with a small duffel bag.

Bemused, she stepped out of the car. When Jason unlocked the cottage door, she hesitated and looked down at her muddy feet. "My shoes."

"Leave them by the door."

As she scuffed them off, he brushed the twigs and grass from the back of her shirt. When she turned, he reached for a piece of straw near her collarbone, and his hand touched her neck. His fingers were warm on her flesh. Neither of them moved.

"I feel as if you've brought me here before," she whispered.

"No. We've never been here." Jason turned away quickly and pushed the door open. "We'd better go in."

Noel nodded.

He stepped back and she followed him into a small sitting room. It fulfilled the promise of the exterior. The upholstered furniture was overstuffed and bright with flowered pillows. The tables, chairs and cabinet pieces were highly polished pine. A simple rag rug decorated the wide boards of the floor. Nothing was dusty or dirty. In fact, it looked as if a meticulous housewife had gone down to the village to fetch a few groceries for her expected visitors.

"Did someone get this place ready for us?"

"My boss keeps several houses like this around the country. They're always ready for occupancy."

"That sounds expensive."

"He can afford it."

She might have asked another question, but as Noel watched Jason carry the cases toward the stairs, the image of coming here before skittered into her head again. Except this time she knew it wasn't a memory. This time she realized her mind was flirting with the idea of a man and a woman alone in a charming honeymoon cottage. A man and a woman who had just kissed each other as if—

As if what?

The silent question was immediately followed by a feeling of longing so intense that she sucked in an audible breath. She knew he heard, because he turned and looked at her. Their eyes locked, and she wondered if he was thinking the same thing as she.

Then he jerked away and began to rapidly ascend the stairs. When she joined him on the second floor, she found that there were two bedrooms. Jason put her luggage in the larger room, which was dominated by a double bed with a high, carved headboard. Then he set his own duffel bag across the narrow hall in a smaller chamber with a single bed.

When he turned, he almost bumped into Noel, who was standing awkwardly in the hall. She stepped back. So did he.

"I—uh—expect you want to get cleaned up," Jason said, gesturing toward the bathroom at the end of the hall. "And there should be a first-aid kit in the medicine cabinet, if you have any scrapes that need attention."

"Thanks." She heard the uncertainty in her own voice.

"I'll be downstairs if you want anything."

He turned and left her standing in the hall. And all at once it hit her how far she'd dropped her guard. My God, what was the matter with her? Being alone with Jason in this place had lulled her into a feeling of safety. And that

was dangerous, she thought as she stepped into her room
and closed the door.

JASON STOOD at the foot of the stairs, listening to the
sounds behind Noel's closed door. He could picture her
opening her luggage and getting out clean clothing. He
wanted to go back up, take her back in his arms and tell
her something that would wipe away the look of mis-
trust that had surfaced in her eyes. But what the hell was
he going to say?

His shoulders sagged as he walked into the sitting
room. He was going to have to report in to Sir Douglas.
And whatever he said to the Sovereign would have to be
factually accurate, because there were ways to check his
story. On the other hand, there were several personal details he was certainly going to leave out. The most important thing he had to do was convince Frye that Noel
was no more than a pawn in this new game—a pawn who
had to be protected while she was useful.

After bringing the guns in from the car and stowing
them in his room, he placed a call to an unlisted number
in Glasgow and waited while the computer linked up with
the secure line to Castle Lockwood.

"Problems?" his employer asked the moment Jason
had identified himself.

"How can you tell?"

"It's the only reason you'd be ringing up."

"Nothing I can't handle."

A note of tension overlaid the older man's voice. "The
lass arrived on schedule?"

"Yes. Then she was scooped up by the authorities at
customs."

"Why?" The sharp question was like the quick thrust
of a rapier.

"I don't know yet."

"But you got her away from them."

"Not me. One of Montgomery's operatives."

Jason listened through several seconds of shocked curses. "I didn't think that old weasel had the nerve to go on the offensive."

"It means he's desperate. Which makes him more dangerous than ever. I think he wanted the girl frightened enough to cooperate with him."

"Aye." There was a long silence on the other end of the line. "Perhaps you shouldn't bring her directly here."

"Then you want to put plan B into effect?" Jason asked, gripping the phone cord in his fingers while he waited for the answer.

"Yes."

Jason let out the breath he'd been holding.

"I don't like surprises. Keeping the lass under control is critical."

"I can take care of that."

"I'll do what I can to help from this end," Frye added.

"What?"

"I'd like to see how you handle things as they develop. Ring me this evening and let me know if there's anything different in the way the lass is reacting."

Before Jason could ask what *that* was supposed to mean, the line went dead. With a silent curse of his own, Jason hung up.

NOEL FOUND ONE of the dresses she'd packed and took it into the bathroom. She washed quickly, inspecting her body for bruises and scrapes which she doused with strong-smelling disinfectant.

The medicine's pungent smell and sting helped dispel the lingering fog that filled her head.

Noel had slipped on her dress and was towel drying her hair when she stopped suddenly. Had she heard voices downstairs? Stepping out into the hall, she listened intently. Jason was talking to someone in a tone too soft for her to make out what he was saying. The one-sided conversation continued, and she guessed he was using the phone.

Quietly she crept toward the stairs and leaned over the railing, but she still couldn't catch more than a blur of low words. Then a phrase leaped out at her. "Then you want to put plan B into effect?"

Noel went very still. Plan B. She didn't know what that meant, but it sounded as if Jason was getting his orders from someone—and he wasn't telling her who. In the car, she'd stupidly asked if he was a guardian angel. What a naive fool she'd been. Jason Zacharias was a dangerous man who had cleverly trapped her upstairs in an isolated cottage. And she'd better find a way to tip the odds a bit in her favor.

On tiptoe she crossed the hall and stepped into the smaller bedroom. Jason must have put his luggage away—probably in the cupboard. When she threw open the doors, the first things she saw were the two guns he'd taken from the truck driver.

She winced and started to back away. Then she told herself it was counterproductive to be intimidated by the weapons. Dropping to her knees, she opened the zipper of the duffel bag he'd shoved into the bottom of the cabinet.

Carefully she began to poke through the contents, trying not to change the position of anything. The luggage held the expected articles. Neatly folded underwear. Jeans. Sweaters. Shirts. Socks. A shaving kit.

It was strangely unsettling to be touching such personal items. Ignoring the feeling, she continued her search. Under some sweat clothes was a flat leather folder. With a little stab of guilt, Noel worked it to the surface and spread it open.

Inside were two dark blue passport booklets with the familiar U.S. eagle crest on the outside. The first one was issued in the name of Jason Zacharias. The picture was recent. His birthplace was listed as Baltimore. His current address was in Chicago. And he was supposed to be a salesman.

Noel snorted. That fit Mr. Zacharias about as well as a tuxedo would fit an alligator.

Why did he need two passports? Was he traveling under an alias when it suited him?

Noel opened the second booklet. As she looked down at the photograph, she felt the blood drain out of her head. To her astonishment she found she was gazing at her own face. It wasn't quite as recent as Jason's picture. In fact, it had been taken two years ago when she'd first gotten a college ID.

As she scanned the rest of the information, she felt her mouth go dry. Her birthdate and place of birth were correct.

But according to this supposedly official U.S. document, she also lived in Chicago. And her name—both in print and as a signature—was Noel Zacharias.

Chapter Five

Noel dropped the passport as if it might explode in her hand.

Noel Zacharias.

That meant... it said... she was Mrs. Jason Zacharias.

Like a cork popping to the surface of a troubled sea, a tantalizing picture sprang into her mind. A bedroom. Dim lights. Soft music. Herself and Jason. Naked. In a double bed. Fevered bodies locked in a tight, urgent embrace. Mouths seeking. Hands moving, caressing, giving pleasure. Words murmured in the darkness.

"Finally you're mine."

"I always have been."

Noel wrapped her arms around her shoulders. Her eyelids drifted closed as the images and the words sent a shiver across skin still warm from the shower. In that one unguarded moment, she ached with every fiber of her being to hold on to the scene. Long ago she'd been in Jason Zacharias's arms. Later she'd spun fantasies about him when she hadn't been capable of coping with a real man in her life. But she had no claims on him. Now it was dangerous even to play with the possibility.

She opened her eyes again, picking up the incriminating document, recognizing it as some kind of cruel hoax.

Noel Zacharias wasn't her name. She was Noel Emery. Deliberately, almost ruthlessly, she called up the details of her life. She lived in Baltimore, not Chicago. She was a paralegal working in the law office of Laura Roswell at 43 Light Street. She drove a red, secondhand Toyota. She rented an apartment in the old house her friend Jo O'Malley owned in Roland Park. She liked to make lunchtime visits to Lexington Market with its fresh produce and ethnic food stalls. She was a frequent patron of the Roland Park Library. And she knew a lot about antique jewelry.

The signature on the passport swam in front of her eyes. She brought it into focus. It looked like her handwriting. That was the way she'd make the *Z* in Zacharias. But Noel Emery had never written that name. It was an elaborate forgery.

But why? Where had Jason gotten it? And how was he planning to use it?

Noel pictured herself scrambling off the floor, going downstairs and waving the thing in his face.

But what was she supposed to say? "I've been searching through your luggage for incriminating evidence and found something strange I'd like you to explain."

At the thought, hysterical laughter bubbled up in her throat. Clasping her hand over her mouth, she shot a glance toward the door and forced herself to choke the noise off.

Grimly she tried to make her mind work with its old, sharp logic. She couldn't picture herself telling Jason how she'd found the passport. Nor was she capable of playing a cat-and-mouse game with him, either. Not in her present state. Which left her only one real alternative: she was going to have to get out of here, and fast.

She looked uncertainly at the document clenched in her fingers. She might as well take this thing with her, because her own passport was still in the hands of the customs authorities.

She tiptoed back across the hall. After slipping into clean shoes, she pulled on her jacket and stuffed the passport into her purse. But it was impossible to keep her hands from shaking. She was alone in a foreign country. The police were looking for her, and a man named Montgomery was sure she was a smuggler. Jason Zacharias probably thought the same thing.

A frisson slithered up Noel's spine as she regarded her luggage. There was a package in her flight bag that didn't belong to her. A package she'd been asked to bring to England. The jewelry. Good Lord, was *that* what they all wanted?

Noel pulled out the small velvet-lined pouch. Then she hesitated. Would she be in worse trouble by bringing it along? Without debate she stuffed the carrying case into her purse. The first thing she'd do after she got away was call her PI friend Jo O'Malley and tell her what had happened. She'd know what to do.

But first she had to escape.

Noel's gaze flicked to the windows. They were probably too small for her to wiggle through. However, the ones in Jason's room were bigger.

When she looked out, she saw there was only a short drop to the roof of a small addition that protruded from the main structure. At least she wouldn't have to make it to the ground in one fell swoop.

After securing the shoulder strap of her purse across her chest, she began to climb through the window frame. She was halfway out when disaster struck.

One moment she was in control, her mind and body focused on escape. The next, she was dizzy, disoriented, and unable to make her limbs work properly.

Chaos

Oh, God. It was one of the accursed attacks. Why did they always seem to come at the worst possible moments?

Please, no. Not . . . now. . . .

This time was different; her silent entreaty was vaporized by a blinding explosion that went off like a magnesium flare in the tissues of her brain.

For several seconds Noel was paralyzed by the totally unexpected agony. Then the white-hot pain made her sink down against the window frame, her fingers unfeeling as they gripped the wood. At first, nothing existed in the universe besides the almost unbearable agony. No thoughts. No sight. No sound.

Then, instinctively, her hands moved. Blindly she reached toward the front of her body, tearing at the tight band that constricted her chest. Lifting the strap over her head, she flung her pocketbook away. It landed on the floor, popping open and spilling its contents in a wide arc.

A moan welled up in her throat as she began to pull at her hair and claw at the spot where her scalp had been stitched together—as if there were some way she could let the demons out of her head. Then, when it seemed the pain was going to drive her insane, the red hot spikes in her skull began to cool.

For a moment, Noel lay across the windowsill panting, feeling a cold wind on her face and something hard and flat digging into her ribs. Struggling to sit, to escape from the terrible prison of her own body, she slipped back through the window into the room, landing with a thud on the floor.

Unaware of her surroundings, she was caught and held by a kaleidoscope of disjointed sensory input forming and reforming deep in the hidden folds of her mind.

Ghostly images. Wavering shapes. Half-articulated words.

A screeching parrot. The aroma of meat roasting over glowing coals. A stretch of moonlit beach. A man's hand stroking her breasts, making her tremble with need.

As the impressions shifted, her body went from hot to icy cold and back again.

Her emotions zinged from desperate wanting to terror and beyond.

Shadow images.

Were they real? Or merely illusions?

The world as a blinding flash of orange. A leaf drifting on gently rolling water. The rich scent of almond-roasted coffee. The moon again. Huge and round, rising over the crest of a mountain. But the scene felt wrong, as if it were enclosed like a snapshot in a silver frame.

Suddenly she was in the picture, wearing a mint green dress that draped softly around her body.

Like Jason's arm. He was there, too. Wearing his marine uniform. Uniform? No, that wasn't right. The dark sports jacket and gray slacks weren't military.

A smile flickered around her lips. He was so handsome. And she looked so healthy and happy. They made a beautiful couple.

Yet as she stared at the people in the picture, sadness replaced the feeling of well-being. They were trapped. Unable to move. At the mercy of—

"Let us go," she whispered.

From out of nowhere, a magic wand waved itself in front of the photograph, releasing the two lovers from their frozen pose. The woman grinned, wiggling her bare feet, feeling the warm sand of the beach squishing pleasantly between her toes and breathing the flower-scented tropical air.

The man laughed, sounding so free that she felt as if her heart would burst. She turned eagerly toward him, and his arms came up to shield her like a solid wall.

"Jason?"

"I'm right here."

Not on the tropical beach. On the shore of a lake. Holding hands, breathing the clean mountain air. Noel tried desperately to hang on to the scene. It was the one she wanted.

But she couldn't keep it from dissolving.

She gave a little moan when she realized he wasn't next to her anymore. He was far away along the shore. He was screaming at her. Waving his arms, shouting a warning. And she didn't know what he meant.

An explosion. The blinding light. His face cut and bleeding. Her own pain. Filling her mind again.

"No," Noel gasped, covering her eyes with her arm, warding off the terrible certainty that everything she wanted most in life had just been snatched away from her.

She lay on the hard floor panting, beating her hands against the wide boards. Fighting off the horrible image.

Her will was strong. She made the frightening picture dissolve like mist burning off in the sun. It was quickly replaced by another.

A different heat. Slick bodies locked in a tight, urgent embrace. Mouths sealed together. Hands caressing, building heat.

"Noel? Where the hell are you?"

His voice. The same, but different.

She tried to answer. Failed.

"Noel?"

She blinked. He was on the floor beside her, gathering her close. Scooping her up in his arms. She was vaguely surprised that this scene didn't wink away like all the rest.

She smoothed her hand across his shoulder. Hard muscles. Yielding flesh. Real. And the wonder of it almost took her breath away. "I wanted it so much. And you're really here!"

"What are you talking about?"

She smiled her secret smile. "I brought you back. Now everything's all right."

He stopped as if caught in a freeze-frame; even the rise and fall of his chest had come to a halt. For an unguarded moment, the look of relief on his face took her own breath away. "Noel."

When he carried her to the rocking chair and sat down, she rested her head dreamily against his chest, profoundly reassured by the beating of his heart. It was rapid at first. Then she felt it slow to a more normal pace.

"Noel, tell me what happened."

At first there were no words to describe it. But as she looked up into his eyes, everything became clear. Or at least, everything that she needed to know.

"Jason."

Jason tried to catch his breath as he stared down into the trusting depths of Noel's eyes.

"Jason," she repeated.

When she said his name like that, he felt as if some tender, hidden core inside himself was tearing apart.

"Take it easy, sweetheart. What happened? Is it your head again?"

She nodded solemnly.

He swore under his breath, struggling to control his anger. She didn't need this. "Does it hurt?"

"Not now."

She looked so peaceful. She didn't seem to be concerned at all that he'd come in and found her sprawled on the floor under the open window of his room.

But her hair was disheveled. He'd heard her scream— and the sound of fists beating against the floor.

He took her hands in his, turning them so he could see the edges. They were an angry red.

"It's all right," she murmured.

There was nothing he could do but gather her close, rock her in the chair. But at the same time his perceptive gaze flicked around the room. It came to rest on the purse that lay on the floor. The bag was open, and the contents were strewn across the wide boards. The first thing he saw was a small zippered pouch. The jewelry? She must have taken it out of her carry-on luggage.

He could see her wallet, too. And a blue passport folder. His brow wrinkled. Wouldn't customs have taken that away from her as soon as they'd picked her up for questioning?

His gaze shot to the gaping cupboard and the unzipped duffel bag. He felt his nerve endings prickle.

While he'd been talking on the phone downstairs, Noel had been quietly going through his things, trying to figure out why he was here and what he was up to. And she'd found the passport.

He knew if he looked he'd find that the one lying on the floor wasn't the document she'd gotten from the State Department. It was the one Sir Douglas Frye had purchased from a very reliable but illegal contact in Zurich.

His mind went through the same steps hers must have taken, and he thought he understood what had happened. Or some of it, anyway. Noel had been on her way out the window. She'd been trying to get away without his finding out. She didn't trust him.

So why was she snuggling so peacefully in his lap?

"Noel?"

"Umm?"

"You found the passport."

"Mrs. Noel Zacharias."

"Yes."

She shifted, tipping her face up toward his. "Why did you leave me in Baltimore after we got married?"

The breath turned to a solid mass in his lungs. "Married?" He could only manage the one word.

"Five years ago. I remember it, sort of."

A pulse had begun to pound in his throat.

"You . . . left me at . . . at my mother's house."

He couldn't speak. He could only stare at her as her lips began to tremble.

"Dangerous . . . assignment." The words were jerky and mechanical, as if she were reading blurry cue cards. "You . . . you told me the . . . marines were sending you to . . . Latin America . . . and it would be safer if I stayed with my mother. You promised you'd come back when it was all over. But you never did." Her voice picked up conviction as she got further into the explanation. "I—I had to get a job with Laura Roswell. I didn't tell her I was married because I didn't want to put you in danger."

His hands tightened on her arms as if he could anchor himself in a world that had suddenly tipped 180 degrees. Married! What did she think she was remembering?

"If we're married, where did we go on our honeymoon?" he managed.

Again there was a moment's hesitation. "A tropical island. A beautiful room. With a balcony overlooking the beach. Palm trees. We made love all night...." Her face took on a dreamy look as if she were remembering a very precious experience. Slowly her hand traced the line of his chin and then his mouth. Stretching to breach the inches that separated their faces, she softly brushed her lips against his.

He didn't respond. Couldn't let himself.

But as she settled back against his chest, his throat was so constricted he could hardly breathe.

"We're finally together again. Oh, Jason."

If only—oh, God, if only—

He closed his eyes, struggling with emotions he'd told himself he'd come to terms with years ago. He'd made choices about his life—his goals. He'd known what he was giving up and why. But the reality of the beautiful, desirable woman in his arms was tearing all his carefully acquired control to shreds.

Mercifully Noel seemed unaware of the turmoil seething in his chest.

"This is like a second honeymoon. We're going to have some time to ourselves in England. And then we're going to Scotland to visit your friend, Sir Douglas Frye. It's going to be fun staying in a real castle."

"Sir Douglas! Where did you get that name?"

She looked perplexed. "Didn't you tell me? Yes. You told me about him before we left Baltimore. I guess he's

not exactly your friend. He's your boss. You like working for him. And now I'm going to get to meet him.''

Jason swore under his breath as an important piece of
the puzzle dropped into place. On the phone Frye had
said—

Not much. Just a promise that he was going to make
sure Noel was cooperative. Now...*this*. Oh, God, *this*.

He struggled to square terrible speculation with reality. Sir Douglas Frye had resources beyond the imagin-
ings of ordinary mortals. Playing mind games was one of
his greatest pleasures. Was there some way the man was
reaching out from his lair in Scotland and controlling
Noel's thoughts? And was he doing more than playing
with Noel's head? Was this another chance to put Jason
Zacharias to the test?

Jason gazed down into her trusting face, trying to reason it all out—and trying to come to grips with the words
that had been popping out of her mouth like bubbles
perking to the surface of a soap pipe.

When he'd rescued her from Montgomery's thug,
she'd been glad to see him. Then she'd been wary. And a
few minutes ago she'd been on her way out the window.
Now here was this strangely detailed story about two of
them getting married five years ago and honeymooning
on a tropical island. It was as if someone had concocted
a fantasy and inserted it into her head like a false memory.

She stirred in his arms. Murmuring something mean-
ingless but soothing, he tucked her face against his
shoulder. He couldn't cope with what he saw in those
eyes. Or his own reluctant conclusions.

Cold sweat bloomed on his skin as he thought about
mind-altering techniques and the little Noel had told him
about her symptoms. She'd said she was still dizzy and

disoriented. That was bad enough. This was a hell of a lot worse.

The fear that rose in his throat was almost paralyzing. My God, what had that bastard Sir Douglas Frye done to her? And how had he done it? Hating to look below the surface, he forced himself to examine the possibilities.

Brainwashing?

No. There couldn't have been enough time for that. Besides, Noel hadn't been in Frye's captivity—as far as he knew.

Subliminal persuasion?

There would have to be some kind of transmitter. And why was it only affecting Noel?

Hypnotic suggestions?

That was a possibility. Perhaps while she'd been in the hospital someone very quick and skillful could have laid the groundwork. The passport could have been the trigger.

It didn't even have to have been in the hospital, he realized suddenly. What about that psychologist, Dr. Franklin? Had she betrayed her friend for a fat fee from Frye? It didn't seem likely from the background reports he'd seen on the woman. She was rich. She didn't need that kind of money. Which left him to the theory he'd been avoiding. What if this had something to do with Frye's secret research labs in Zurich?

A new, more tangible wave of fear washed over him, and his hands tightened on Noel's arms.

"What?"

"I'm sorry. It's all right," he croaked. With a shaky hand, he stroked her hair and felt her settle against him again.

Jason's mind scrambled to recall the confidential report he'd seen. According to his sources, Sir Douglas was funding biotech experiments conducted by some underground Swiss laboratories.

The researchers had started by implanting artificial-intelligence devices in animals to alter their natural behavior. And there were hints that human experiments were going to be the next step. He hadn't paid attention to the fine print because the whole idea had repulsed him.

Jason looked down at Noel. When she shifted her head and smiled back, his stomach knotted. My God, was Frye using her as some sort of human guinea pig? Had it amused him that he was giving one of his favorite operatives a little bonus in the bargain?

All at once, he had to struggle to keep from gagging.

Noel must have seen the expression that crossed his face.

"What's wrong?"

"I—"

She laid a gentle hand on his cheek. "It's—it's all right. About your leaving. You did what you had to do. What you thought was best. For my safety. And I understand. I've already said I forgive you."

A spasm racked his chest, and his hand clenched and unclenched on the arm of the chair.

"Jason. Please."

He tried to speak but couldn't manage it.

There was a subtle change in her smile. "Now that we're together again, don't you want to make love to me?"

Chapter Six

Every muscle in Jason's body went rigid.

Oh, yes. Oh, God, yes.

Somehow he kept the answer from spilling out of his mouth. His traitorous gaze shot to the very serviceable bed five feet from where they were sitting. No, on second thought, it was too narrow. When he made love to her he'd want room to—

He canceled the idea before it had more than half formed. Yet he couldn't stop his body from reacting to her words—and the sensual images they evoked. Standing up abruptly, he tumbled a startled Noel off his lap, catching her and setting her on her feet before she landed in a heap on the floor.

"Sorry."

She giggled. "You're in a hurry."

"Sweetheart, w-we have to talk about some things. I mean, before we—" His mouth was so dry he could hardly get the words out.

"If it's important to you."

"Yes."

Talk. That might get him through the next hour, but what about tonight? He didn't let himself think about the two of them isolated in this cozy little cottage, cosseted by the darkness of an English country night. Alone and both wanting—

Sir Douglas had made him a present of his most secret fantasy. But there was no way he could accept the gift.

He tugged on Noel's hand. "Come on, let's go outside. The fresh air will do us both good."

She nodded.

As he led her downstairs, she gave his hand a warm squeeze, and he felt a matching contraction in his chest.

They crossed the small sitting room and stepped outside into a garden blooming with tulips and daffodils. Stone paths wound between the flower beds, which alternated with clumps of fragrant herbs and neatly trimmed bushes.

"I love this place. It's so pretty—and so private," Noel murmured. "How did you ever find it?"

He jerked his mind back from the dangerous path down which it had been wandering. "I didn't. It belongs to Sir Douglas."

"I'll have to thank him for lending it to us."

Jason snorted.

"I thought you liked working for him."

"I'm considering making a change," he growled, then stopped in his tracks as the implications of the angry remark came home to him. Anything he said to Noel might be repeated right back to Frye.

"Is that what you want to discuss?"

"No. And I was only kidding. There's no better man to work for than Sir Douglas." The accolade almost stuck in his throat.

They walked slowly through a hedge trained into the shape of an archway and stood staring out across the impossibly green fields. Such a peaceful scene. Like the last safe place in a nightmare just before everything twists and the demons come. Except that in this case, there was only one demon. Sir Douglas Frye.

Jason stole a glance at Noel. She looked so happy. So glad to be with him, as if her heart was beating to the exact same rhythm as his. The temptation to pull her into his arms and press her body against his made his hands tremble and the blood pound through his veins. He fought the fierce elemental longings. He couldn't take advantage of her like that. Not and keep what was left of his self-respect.

Which put him on one hell of a slippery slope. He was already on the way down, and he could feel himself picking up momentum.

He closed his eyes. Back in Baltimore the situation had seemed untenable. It became more impossible with every passing minute. He didn't want to think about the Zurich project. But he had to, if he had a hope of finding a way out of this mess. In the early experiments, the animals had been controlled by electrodes inserted into their brains. Electrodes that received certain signals and which modified behavior. Later, miniaturized computer circuitry had been substituted.

His legs stopped carrying him forward and he came to a jerky stop. Noel paused, too.

"Jason, I can tell something's bothering you. I know we haven't spent that much time together. But we made a commitment to each other when we got married. And if we're going to make a new start, we should be open with each other."

Tiger claws ripped at his insides.

"You have to share your problems with me," she finished in a pleading voice.

He cursed softly under his breath as he did what he'd been wanting to do all along. He pulled Noel to himself, wrapping her tightly in his embrace.

She sighed and stirred against him, and he felt unleashed arousal shoot through him like a bolt of lightning. Unable to help himself, he gave in to the pleasure of sliding his hands down her waist and hips, and cupping her bottom.

As he pressed her body against his, she made a joyful little sound in her throat and nuzzled her warm lips against his neck.

The need to dip his head, to cover her lips with his was like a fire blazing up inside him. Somehow he stopped himself from doing it. With trembling hands, he began to comb his fingers through her hair, looking for the spot where she'd been injured.

"That feels so nice," she murmured.

When he found the scar, he went very still. "What's this?" He could hear the hoarseness in his own voice.

"Where I hurt my head. When my uncle—" She swallowed. "When Uncle Henry was killed, my scalp was split."

"The men who killed your uncle bashed you on the head," he said, deliberately shedding the warmth of the mood.

Her fingers dug into his arm. He took a step back so that her hand and his sweater were the only point of contact.

"You needed stitches."

"Yes. I guess you never saw the wound because I was already out of the hospital and staying at Abby's when you came back." She stretched out an arm toward him. "I needed you so much, and there you were."

Jason couldn't speak; he could only nod. That was what Sir Douglas Frye made Noel believe. Unable to face the trust shining in her eyes, he turned and stalked back toward the house.

He heard Noel call his name, but he didn't stop walking away from her.

Damn Frye. Damn him to hell. He'd seen her head wound, all right, although he couldn't tell that to Noel. He'd seen it minutes after it had been inflicted. Then he'd been worried about concussion and brain injury. He hadn't been thinking that her split scalp had opened up a golden opportunity for Sir Douglas Frye, the man who was a master of manipulating people. The Sovereign was always looking for new ways to control his victims. Probably he'd been planning a test of his new electronic toy for months. What was it? A wafer-thin computer chip? He wanted to scream his rage. He kept his teeth clamped together. Had Noel just been in the wrong place at the wrong time? Or had Sir Douglas singled her out for special attention?

Jason felt his own scalp crawl. Frye had known since November that Henry Marconi wanted out of the organization. Which meant he would have dug up every piece of useful data in Marconi's background. And he'd certainly have gotten a detailed report on his beautiful niece.

How long, exactly, did it take to come up with a full set of false memories tailor-made to a particular individual? Were they just pictures in her mind? Or did they include sounds and tastes and smells?

And was Marconi the only reason Frye had focused on Noel? Jason's hands clenched into fists. Picking up one of the loose paving stones from the path, he flung it toward the wall of the cottage.

WITH A HEARTSICK FEELING of emptiness, Noel stared at her husband's rapidly departing back. He'd turned and walked away from her. What had she said or done to upset him?

She wasn't sure whether to follow or to leave him alone for a while. Uncertainly, she made her way back to the garden. But once inside the hedge, she came to a halt. The Jason Zacharias she remembered was warm and loving. Sometimes this man was like that. Then he'd shut her out as though an iron gate had dropped between them. Hurt and confused, she sank down onto the stone bench near the archway and sat with her shoulders hunched.

It was so frustrating. Not just Jason. Herself. When she tried to think things through, everything was so muddled up inside her head. Sometimes her memories were sharp and clear. When she thought about school or Dad leaving, or her college courses, there was no problem. With other recollections, it was like trying to see the road through an icy windshield. Everything was blurry and indistinct. Except that something was suddenly different just now. When she'd strained to come up with replies to Jason's questions, the answer had popped into her head like the Ping-Pong balls in a lottery machine.

With trembling fingers she reached up and touched the place where she'd been hit on the head. She'd been fine until the injury. Since then—

Did she have a brain injury that the doctors hadn't detected? Or was everybody lying to her about the real situation? Was that why Jason had come back and taken her off on this second honeymoon trip?

The fear gripped her by the throat and came out as a quavery plea for help. "Jason—"

She didn't know she'd gasped his name aloud until he was beside her on the bench, turning her toward him, enfolding her in the safety of his arms as if he hadn't run away from her a little while ago.

"What is it? What's wrong?"

She buried her face in the scratchy wool of his sweater. She didn't want to ask any of the questions chasing each other around in her mind, but she had to know. "Am I dying? Is that what you're so worried about? Did that crack on my head cause some damage—or did it make me crazy?" The last part came out as a little sob.

He swore roughly. "No."

She looked up pleadingly into his face. "You wouldn't lie to me, would you?"

"You're not dying! And you're not crazy!"

"Then why do I feel so—so—odd?"

"Tell me what you feel."

She tried to put it into words. "Sometimes I feel like I'm absolutely sure of everything, and I know who I am and who we are. Then with no warning, I'm not certain of anything." Her hands fluttered. "No, that's not right. I'll have a memory, and I don't know if it's the right one. Does that make any sense?"

"Yes."

"I'm so scared." The admission was barely above a whisper. Anxiously she watched his face for any sign that he was hiding the truth.

"I wish you hadn't been in your uncle's shop when those hoods came in."

"But it brought you back to me."

"Yes." His jaw was rigid for several seconds. "And now we'll get through this together."

She clung to the reassurance in his voice as she tightened her arms around his neck and clung to his strong, solid body. "I love you so much. I'm so glad to have you back."

"Everything's going to be okay. I promise."

JASON HELD NOEL protectively against his chest for long moments, because he didn't dare let her see the moisture gathering in his eyes. She had been through so damn much in her short life. And now this! When he finally had control of himself, he slung his arm around her shoulders and led her back to the house.

"We probably ought to see what we can put together for dinner."

"Dinner! I wasn't even thinking. Are you hungry?"

"Yeah," he lied. Getting a meal on the table would occupy them while he figured out what the hell to do about the device he was sure was implanted under her scalp. What he really needed to know was the scope of the thing's control. How much could Noel reason with the chip in place. And exactly what memories were being forced onto her without her consent. And why.

As they checked the larder, Jason made a monumental effort to keep the conversation light, giving Noel a chance to feel comfortable with him while he tried to determine what she thought was her real past and what wasn't.

"There's lamb chops in the fridge," he called out from behind the open door.

"No. Not after seeing all those cute little lambs in the fields." She was taking stock of the pantry. "Are you going to be happy with canned soup? They've got split pea and chicken noodle."

"Split pea. We can have it with cheese. There's some real English cheddar. And some white grapes."

"And crackers." Noel pulled out a box. "Only they're called biscuits."

Jason set the fruit in the sink and turned on the tap.

"Where did you get your paralegal degree?" he asked above the sound of the running water.

"Villa Julie. They have a great program. And I got a partial scholarship."

"I'll bet you did real well."

"Top ten percent of my class." The pride in her eyes faded. "Laura had to hire someone to take over for me after—"

"You'll be one hundred percent in no time at all," Jason soothed, cursing himself for introducing a subject that was going to disturb her.

He let Noel set the table while he stared at the thick green soup he was stirring. What was it like to have some outside force stirring up your thoughts and your emotions, making you do things that were diametrically opposed to your own best interests? Turning lies into truth and twisting reality until it was unrecognizable. Big Brother. Right in your head.

He had to stop himself from striding into the other room, grabbing Noel by the shoulders and trying to explain it to her. But if he gave in to the impulse to ease his conscience, Frye would have access to every word he said to her. The only way to keep the Sovereign in the dark was to take the damn controller out of her head.

Would all the mental disturbances go away if the implant was removed? Or was that precisely the wrong thing to do? For starters, he was no surgeon. And he didn't have all the details from Zurich.

Suppose he did get the damn thing out? When they got to Castle Lockwood, wouldn't Frye want to make sure his new toy was still in place? How was his trusted operative going to explain a fresh incision in Noel's scalp?

God, what a set of choices to face. Jason closed his eyes, feeling self-doubt twisting in his vitals like a piece of barbed wire.

"Is the soup ready?" Noel came up behind him and put a hand lightly on his shoulder.

He had to keep from going into a defensive posture. "Yeah. Get the bowls."

As Noel opened one of the cabinets, he quickly exited the kitchen, snatching up the plate of cheese and crackers on his way out the door.

He stopped short when he entered the dining alcove. She'd put fresh daffodils in a vase and found candles somewhere. Their flickering light was an added touch of warmth. Well, maybe they'd help hide his expressions, since he was having a hell of a time controlling his emotions.

When Noel came through to the dining alcove, he was safely ensconced on the other side of the gateleg table.

She set down the two bowls and pulled out the chair opposite him. They both unfolded napkins and began to eat, but Jason couldn't work up much enthusiasm for the food. And it looked as if Noel's appetite was about as meager as his.

After a couple of bites, Jason set down his spoon and toyed with one of the crackers. He'd been racking his brain trying to think of a devious way to assess her condition. Maybe a direct approach would be better.

"You say you're having problems with certain memories. What about if you describe something to me, something that we both remember. We can see if the recollections match."

"Yes." She took a deep breath. "Probably the thing we'd both remember best is our honeymoon."

He didn't trust himself to speak as he regarded her in the flickering candlelight. She was so beautiful, so desirable and so glad to be with him. In turn he could feel the need for her seeping through him.

Her face took on a dreamy look as she waited for him to say something. When he didn't, she continued. "It was so nice of Uncle Henry to give us that week in Jamaica."

So that's how a marine corporal was supposed to have afforded a tropical vacation.

"I was so shy. Because I knew you were experienced and I—I hadn't been with anyone else before." She reached across the table and covered his hand with hers. "So you took me to dinner at that restaurant on the beach. We had champagne. Then you asked the band to play a string of slow songs. And we danced out on the patio. There wasn't anyone else outside. Just us in the moonlight. You held me close, and told me how much you loved me—" her voice faltered momentarily "—and stroked my back, and kissed my hair, and my ear, and my neck."

While she spoke, he had turned his hand palm up. As if they had a will of their own, his fingers began to move against hers. The memory wasn't something he shared. But she was making him feel the scene—the two of them together, warm and close—making him long for the images to be true. He could feel his pulse accelerating wildly. He found the right spot at her wrist and felt hers, too. It was thumping in time with his own.

"You were so sexy. You knew just how to seduce me. By the time the music quit, I wasn't sure I could make it back to our room under my own power." She slid her foot across the floorboards, finding his under the table and pressing. "Do you remember how you closed the door and leaned back against it and held me and started working the zipper down the back of my—

"Stop—"

"Am I telling it right?"

"Why did you pick that particular memory?" he asked thickly.

She brushed her fingers against his, and the contact points were like points of fire, heating his blood. "Because now *I'm* trying to seduce my husband, since he's obviously reluctant to start anything."

He could see she was bravely forcing herself to meet his eyes, and the vulnerability he saw in her face stole his breath. Somehow he managed to make his voice work. "Noel, you didn't have to do that to make me want you."

"Then why are you avoiding getting close to me?"

He pulled his hand away from hers, balling it into a fist. "Because I'm feeling guilty about this situation and about us."

"Jason, you may be my husband and you may have come back to me, but being together again isn't going to work unless you share your feelings with me."

"You're wrong. I'm not your husband."

Chapter Seven

"*What* did you say?"

Noel felt as if she were a tightrope walker whose wire had just been slashed, sending her plummeting into space. But when she saw the look of anguish that spread across Jason's face, she realized she wasn't the only one in pain.

"I mean," he began, his voice raw, "much as I'd like to take advantage of the situation, I don't have the right to claim any of the privileges of being your husband."

"Why not?"

The house was deathly quiet. It had got dark while they'd been sitting at the table, and the candles were the only illumination in the dining alcove. The wavering light accented the harsh lines of his face.

"A husband who leaves his wife is no husband."

"You left because you thought you were protecting me. Now you're back, and we have the chance to start over."

"My life hasn't got any less dangerous," he said.

"Then why are we here together? What's going on?"

At his look of withdrawal, she exploded. "For God's sake, tell me!"

"I can't. I've already said more than I should have."

"You haven't said *anything*. You're just making me more confused."

"I'm sorry. You don't know how sorry."

She waited for him to say something else—to feel something else. Sorry wasn't what she wanted. But his lips were clamped together as though Saint Peter himself couldn't pry them open.

"Well, then..." She didn't know how to break the stalemate. But if he was going to leave things like this, she couldn't sit here and take it any longer. "I'm going to bed."

"Good night."

She wasn't sure what she'd expected. Certainly not that oddly mild, prosaic response. Somehow that was the last straw. Without further word, she headed for the stairs.

Fumbling in her suitcase, she found a nightgown, tossed it onto the bed and went into the bathroom. When she came back, she picked up the gown. It was pale green with little cap sleeves, and made of lightweight cotton. One of her old favorites. But not the sort of thing she would have chosen for a second honeymoon.

Maybe she hadn't had time to buy anything new.

Her brow wrinkled. Wouldn't she remember something like that?

Shrugging, she got undressed and slipped between the covers. But once she'd plumped up the pillow, she realized she couldn't bear the idea of lying alone in the comfortable double bed. Not when she'd been picturing the two of them in it together— She choked off the thought before it could become any more graphic.

But she couldn't prevent tears from gathering behind her eyelids. Tears of hurt. And confusion.

Abruptly she sat up, swung her legs over the side of the bed and stood up. Feeling irrational and downright silly, she tiptoed across the hall and into the other room.

Once inside, Noel stood uncertainly, her eyes moving from the freestanding cupboard to the single bed against the wall and the rocking chair where Jason had held her on his lap when—when what?

She'd been on the floor. In here. Was that right?

Once again, the memory wouldn't come.

In the next instant, as if she—or someone else—had tuned the receiver to a different channel, her mind switched quickly to another topic. When she and Jason had come in, he'd put her things in one room and his in the other. He hadn't intended—he'd been assuming all along that they wouldn't sleep together.

Since they'd been out in the garden and come back inside, she hadn't been thinking at all about their arrival at the cottage. Now it came back to her in vivid detail.

And earlier. He'd chased her across a field. My Lord. It was as if a door in her mind had suddenly opened, flooding a dim corner with illumination. The truck driver. He'd been taking her to someone named—

Named what?

Noel squeezed her eyes shut, trying to bring the earlier part of the day into focus. It seemed like a million years ago. Or like a memory that belonged to someone else.

She and Jason had left Baltimore together. That had to be true because they were here in England now.

As she tried to recall the details, she started to tremble. Yet she simply couldn't picture Jason with her at the ticket counter or in the departure lounge at BWI. She could remember her friend, Abby. Abby had given them a ride. Abby had parked while she'd gone into the terminal. But she couldn't put Jason into the scene.

A pulse was pounding in her temple.

Chaos

The word floated in her mind, bringing a sick, wretched feeling.

She thrust it away and tried to proceed reasonably. All right, she ordered herself, forget about the airport. What about the plane? On the plane, Jason had—

She caught a sudden image of them sitting together on their way to England. Talking about the trip. Laughing. Having a drink before dinner. The picture brought a rush of relief.

Until she tried to remember what they'd talked about and couldn't bring back a single shred of conversation. The in-flight movie was a lot more vivid.

Swaying on her feet, she took several steps forward and landed on the bed. Cold sweat had bloomed on her skin, and she lay there panting for breath.

Another attack.

No. It wasn't the same.

She tried to lie very still, comparing the way she felt now and the way she'd been feeling when she'd had the earlier episodes. Then, she'd imagined her head was a satellite receiver, and a special broadcast was being beamed just to her. This was different. She'd already received the program and stored it on tape. Now her brain was having trouble playing it back correctly.

While she and Jason had been sitting at the table, he'd reassured her about her mental state. Suddenly she felt as if she'd fallen through a crevasse in a glacier—and there was nothing around her but blinding white fear.

Shivering violently, Noel looked toward the door. The terrified, insecure part of her wanted to run back downstairs and seek the protection of her husband's arms—

like in the garden when she'd called out to him. The realist knew the solace would only be temporary.

Needing to hold on to something, Noel gathered up wads of the bedspread and clutched them in her hands. Forcing herself to let go, she slipped under the covers and pulled them up to her chin.

She could hear Jason moving around downstairs, clearing the table, putting dishes into the sink. Running water. So normal and natural sounding. A husband doing the kitchen chores because his wife was feeling ill. But would anything ever be normal and natural again?

THE SOUND OF HARSH voices snapped her from sleep to alertness, every nerve in her body jangling. Men were talking downstairs. One of them was Jason. Was another the person he'd called earlier? Her eyes shot to the window as she remembered the escape attempt. Then her attention was pulled back to the lower floor by the sound of a scuffle. Noel sat up in bed, her heart thumping wildly.

"Where's the girl?"

"Not here. You're too late." Jason's voice was louder than the questioner's. His answer ended in a kind of groan that made Noel go cold all over. Next came a muffled smashing noise like flesh being pounded. This time, there was no reply at all from Jason.

Noel's heart leaped to her throat as she pictured her husband slumped to the floor.

Someone had broken in. What were they doing to Jason? What would they do to *her?*

"He's lying. You watch him. We'll find the bird."

There were more than two of them, Noel realized. Three? Four? How many men would Montgomery send? And how had they known where to find her?

Montgomery?

The name had jumped to the surface of her mind like a fish springing after bait, but she didn't have time to figure out where it had come from. She had to get away before they got her, too.

Someone began moving rapidly around the first floor, opening doors and knocking furniture about. There was no time to think, only to act. Noel leaped out of the bed and ran across the small room. She was in the act of pushing open the window sash when the image of a machine gun sprang into her mind.

Guns. She'd seen them.

Where?

On the shelf of the cupboard.

Turning back, she threw open the door, pulled out the larger of the two weapons and slung the leather strap over her shoulder. Then she wiggled out the window, tearing the sleeve of her gown and scraping her shoulder and hip on the wood in her haste. Ignoring the pain, she listened to the racket of booted feet thumping on the stair treads.

The night was cold and damp. Shivering in her thin gown, Noel moved as far as she could from the window. Flattening herself against the wall of the house, she braced her bare feet on the slanted, gravelly surface. She was on the roof of the one-story extension at the back of the house. Somehow she'd known it would be there and that she wouldn't find herself falling to the ground from the second floor. Just the way she'd known the guns were in the cupboard.

The intruders were across the hall, tossing her luggage around the room like airport baggage handlers gone berserk. Did they think she was hiding in a suitcase?

Then Noel's heart stopped as she heard one of them open the window. If he stuck his head out the window of this room, she was sunk. Her pale skin and pale green nightgown would be a magnet for his gaze.

Her hand clutched the grip of the machine gun. When she'd been taking a course in criminology, one of the guys in the class had been friends with an instructor at the FBI Academy in Quantico, Virginia. He'd arranged for several students to tour the facility. One of the main attractions had been a practice session on the shooting range. So she knew how to use the gun; she wasn't helpless. Yet if she fired the weapon, she'd only get the one man, and the rest of them would know where she was.

Frantically she looked around for someplace to hide and spotted a narrow extension to the roof, hanging out over the edge of the building. Was it strong enough to take her weight?

She didn't have time to test the structural integrity of the building. The ledge groaned as she stepped onto the overhang. Teeth clenched, Noel edged out around the corner, her right foot leading in a sort of awkward shuffle. At the same time, her fingers searched for handholds on the irregular stone wall. She was terrified to look down, but squeezing her eyes shut only made things worse. Grimly she inched as far away from the corner as she could, feeling the machine gun flap against her side. With each step, she waited for the ledge to give way.

Behind her the window opened, and she froze in place, her cheek pressed against a rough piece of sandstone. Was she far enough around the corner? Would the wind blow her gown back where he could see it? She was afraid to move, afraid to breathe, afraid to let go of the wall and pull her skirt tight. There was nothing she could do but wait and pray.

She could feel her fingers tearing loose and knew there were only seconds left before she crashed to the ground.

Then the window slammed again, and the heavy steps receded down the stairs once more.

Noel shifted her hold. As quickly as she could, she made her way back to the solid expanse of the roof and collapsed, panting. But she couldn't stay there. When the men who had Jason didn't find her on their first try, they'd make a more thorough search. She couldn't let them capture her, too. She had to get Jason away from them.

Looking around for a means of escape, Noel spotted an exposed pipe at the corner of the building. Dropping over the edge, she wrapped her legs around the metal tube and slowly lowered herself with her arms. A few moments later, she was on the ground, and it was all she could do to stop herself from running headlong away from the house.

Instead she slid along the wall toward the front, where she could see light streaming out into the darkness through the windows. Concealed by the shrubbery, she made her way to the sill and listened.

"Where is she?"

"Somewhere safe. They left me here as a decoy, moron."

"Don't mess us about, lad." The quiet observation was followed by a thudding noise and then a groan. Noel risked a peek through the lower windowpanes and had to bite into her lower lip to keep from crying out. Three very large and very tough-looking intruders formed a circle around her husband. One held a gun. One held Jason by the arms, and the third was standing in front of him, drawing back his fist. As she watched in horror, he landed a solid punch in the middle of Jason's stomach. It was followed by another to his jaw. He was slammed backward against the man who was holding him, but he stayed on his feet.

"You can do that all night, but I'm not going to tell you where she is," he said in a surprisingly steady voice.

"We'll see about that," the spokesman growled.

"We ain't got all night, Tim," the one with the gun objected, looking nervously out into the darkness as if he thought someone was watching.

Noel froze. But he wasn't facing her.

"What if somebody comes?"

"Shut your bloody trap. Nobody's comin'."

"This ain't workin' out the way it was supposed to," the one who held Jason snarled.

Under the tough exteriors, they all looked worried.

Noel sank back against the wall. My God, they were after *her,* and Jason wasn't telling them anything. If she came around and knocked on the door, they'd have what they wanted. But the thought of delivering herself into their hands made a sick feeling rise in her throat.

What would they do to her? And even more frightening, what would they do to Jason when they found out he'd been lying?

The awful possibilities made Noel's palms clammy with fear, but there was only one way she could think of to save Jason. After wiping her hands on her gown, she released the safety catch on the machine gun. Three against one still weren't very good odds. And they had a hostage, which made it a hundred times worse. She couldn't just burst in there and say, "Put your hands up."

What she needed was a diversion.

Working her way quietly out of the bushes, she stopped at the corner near the front door. She tried to keep from picturing how she looked, barefoot in her nightgown, with an automatic weapon cradled in her arm. Instead, she made sure she remembered the layout of the downstairs.

"Well, here goes nothing," she murmured, and squeezed the trigger. A burst of gunfire shattered the darkness. Noel tried to prepare herself for the kick of the weapon. Still, it pushed her backward, and she had to hold tightly to the cold metal to keep it in her hands.

Then she was racing around to the back door.

She came in through the small kitchen. It was only a few steps to the dining alcove off the living room. Everyone was facing front now, staring in the direction from which the shots had come.

"The house is surrounded," she growled, amazed at how steady her voice sounded. "Drop your weapons and you won't be killed."

Two of the men froze. The one called Tim whirled back toward her, pistol raised.

Chapter Eight

Noel aimed the gun and squeezed the trigger again, vaguely surprised to see red splotches appear on the front of the man's shirt. He sank to the floor. Jason was already moving, wrenching himself from the grasp of the startled man who held him.

He rounded on him, snatching at the pistol stuck in his waistband. There was a muffled shot as they struggled.

From her vantage point at the doorway, Noel had stopped breathing. When Jason straightened, holding the gun, she felt her knees sag.

Two men lay dead or wounded on the floor. The third hadn't waited for a clean sweep. He'd bolted into the night. Jason went after him, and Noel heard more shots ring out.

Amazed that her legs would still hold her erect, she ran across the living room and stepped out, straining to see into the darkness. The two men had vanished, and she waited for what seemed like forever, braced for more gunfire. Relief swept over her when she saw her husband trotting back across the field. He was alone.

"Too much of a head start," he clipped out. His face was flushed and covered with a sheen of perspiration, and he was breathing hard.

"Oh, Jason." Realizing she was still holding the machine gun, Noel propped the weapon against the wall and came toward him. She didn't know which she needed more, to assure herself that he was all right or to feel the tough, supple strength of his body.

He stared into her eyes, his gaze filled with a mixture of shock and confusion—and relief. His head shook almost imperceptibly. Then he crushed her against his chest. "Noel. Oh, Noel."

Wordlessly she clung to him. When she lifted her head, his lowered. Then his lips were molding themselves to hers, moving over hers with desperate urgency.

She kissed him back with the same fervor. He was safe. He was here in her arms, his mouth moving restlessly, possessively, telling her that his need was as great as her own. Strengthening the fragile bond between them. It was the only level of communication that made any sense. She wanted to lose herself in the private world they had created. But Jason brought her back to reality.

"That was a damn crazy stunt," he said roughly. "You could have been killed."

"Those men . . . I saw what they were doing to you—through the window. Are you all right?"

"I've felt better. But I'm more or less in one piece."

She tried to keep the tears in her eyes from spilling down her cheeks.

"I was praying you'd hear what was going on and get out of the house somehow. I tried to stall them, but I was afraid they'd go up and find you in bed."

"Your voice woke me up. I got out the window and went across the roof."

"You should have taken off."

"I couldn't leave you like that." She reached up and gently touched his face where he'd been punched.

"Noel. God, sweetheart. I always knew you were brave."

"You make me brave."

She was still leaning into him. For several heartbeats he kept his arms tightly around her, then he straightened and moved her gently away.

"We've got to leave. The third one could be back with reinforcements."

Noel let Jason turn her around and propel her through the front door, but she stopped short when she stepped into the living room. Two men lay unmoving on the floor. One of them—

She felt her knees turn rubbery. "I killed him."

Jason held her firmly by the elbows. "You did what you had to do—to save your life and mine." He hurried her along the side of the room and up the stairs. "You have two minutes to get dressed."

Noel didn't know whether she made his deadline, but she was sure she set some sort of record for pulling on her clothes while Jason cleared her toilet articles out of the bathroom. She grabbed her suitcase. Jason took the flight bag and his duffel. Both the luggage and the machine gun went in the car with them—the cases in the back seat, the weapon between the two front seats.

As the sedan started down the driveway, Noel felt her tension mount. Was the other man out there in the dark, waiting? She half expected another vehicle to pull out in front of them and block the exit, but none did.

Jason's headlights cut through the blackness as he raced down the country roads.

"Where are we going?"

"First, I'm putting some miles between us and this place. Then we'll find a farm that rents out tourist rooms. Montgomery can't check every B and B in a hundred-mile radius. Unless we're damn unlucky we should be okay for tonight.''

Noel shuddered. ''How did they figure out where we were?''

''I'd give a lot to know. Maybe there's a spy in Sir Douglas's organization. That should give him something to think about.''

Noel took a deep breath and let it out slowly. ''Are you going to tell me why those men came after us?''

He didn't answer right away, and she wrapped her hand around the edge of the seat. ''Jason, I need to know.''

''I'll tell you,'' he ground out. ''As soon as we're safe. But you may be sorry. We both might.''

IT WAS CLOSE to ten when Jason pulled in between the stone gateposts of Still Water Farm, having been directed there by the owner of a pub in the village nearby. Still Water Farm's proprietress, a Mrs. Lancaster, was expecting them.

The car came to a stop in a lighted courtyard between a large stone barn and a two-story house that looked as if it was several centuries old. Noel felt her chest tighten. The ride was over, and Jason had promised to level with her. Had he meant it?

Mrs. Lancaster showed them to a one-room cottage several hundred yards from the main house. It was far less elaborate than the one in which they'd planned to spend the night. Noel watched her husband as he carried the luggage into the bedroom, checked the doors and windows and closed the curtains. In the light from the ancient floor lamp, his chiseled features were thrown into sharp relief against the homespun fabric.

Suddenly self-conscious, Noel stepped into the bathroom and closed the door. When she came out again, Jason was lining up the luggage against the wall beside a tall wardrobe.

He glanced up and met her gaze, and for an instant, neither of them moved. She felt the tension crackling between them. Then he passed her and went into the bathroom. She heard the water running for a long time. Was he stalling, trying to figure out what he was going to say? Or was he afraid she was going to beg him to make love to her again? Well, he didn't have to worry about that. She sighed wearily. She didn't want to risk another rejection, but she was too tired to sit up in a chair.

When Jason opened the door again, Noel was stretched out on the quilt, two pillows propped behind her head and her shoes beside her on the floor. He gave her a long, sweeping glance that made her feel as if she were wearing a sheer negligee rather than a shirt and slacks. Her heart rate quickened, and she thought he might be planning to join her. Instead he settled into one of the faded wing chairs.

"I told you I was going to keep you safe, and I let you down," he said in a strained voice.

Noel resisted the urge to go to him and stroke the tortured look from his face. "You didn't know what to expect," she replied softly. "If we're both prepared, we've got a better chance. That's why I've got to know what's happening. You say we're in danger. From Montgomery? Is Sir Douglas trying to protect us from him?"

"Okay." Jason rubbed a hand across his face. "We'll start with Montgomery. What do you know about him?"

"I guess he sent the men tonight. Probably the guy in the truck, too. And they aren't after you, they're after me." She was hoping he'd come back with a denial.

Instead he nodded. "Yes."

"What did I do?" She heard the bewilderment in her own voice. "Did something happen that I can't remember? Is it because of my uncle?"

She saw Jason's knuckles whiten as his hands gripped the arms of the chair. "Let's see what you *do* remember. If I start trying to explain everything to you, you're not going to believe me."

"Why not?"

"Please. If you insist on doing this, we have to do it my way."

Noel closed her eyes for a moment, her head throbbing. He was asking her to risk something almost as frightening as bursting into the room full of invaders. What was so scary about giving him information? She couldn't explain the fear. She only knew it took every ounce of willpower she possessed to keep from bolting. "What should I tell you? What's important?" she asked.

"Your getting the machine gun out of the cupboard. How did you know it was there?"

"I saw it when...when I searched your suitcases." She stopped and stared at him. "Why would I search your luggage?"

Jason leaned forward, his face tense. "Try to go back. What happened when you got to England?"

Fighting pain and confusion, Noel strained to bring some incident into focus, trying to recall the two of them picking up their luggage or going through customs or getting the rental car. She drew a large, frightening blank.

"I—I guess we did the stuff you usually do when you get to a new country." She gestured vaguely toward their suitcases, hoping he couldn't see how much the lack of details unnerved her.

"Do you remember having some trouble at customs?"

"Trouble?" A chill swept across her skin.

"Think!"

Noel drew back, pressing into the pillows, feeling her head pound. She didn't want to remember. But she had to! Every muscle and nerve in her body strained as if some physical act of strength could haul her out of this mental abyss. And, suddenly, against all hope, a picture flashed into her mind of a stern-looking older man and a tall one about her own age. They were wearing dark blue uniforms.

"Welby," she said in a tentative voice.

"Who's that?"

"The customs inspector. He was—" Noel stopped short, feeling a dull blade slice through her head. She groaned.

Chaos

"What's wrong?"

"It ... hurts ... to think about it."

His voice was tightly controlled. "About what?"

Noel grimaced. She'd been trying to remember, but the half-formed picture had been driven from her head by the pain.

"Maybe this wasn't such a good idea."

"No. I ... want ... to ... remember." Frustrated, she banged her hand against the night table, then had to grab the lamp as it threatened to topple off to the floor.

"Noel—"

"Please. Help me! What was I trying to tell you?"

It was a moment before he answered. "About someone named Welby."

"Welby. Customs." Again a picture of a man in a dark uniform danced in her mind. Gray hair, mustache. Despite the dizziness and panic, she tried to bring him into sharper focus. She was unaware that tears had formed in her eyes until she found her cheeks were wet. Still she wouldn't quit. Hugging her knees, she rocked her body back and forth, forcing the words to come. "He—he thought I was smuggling something. I was so scared. It was like a nightmare. We called Flora, but she wasn't at the house where I was supposed to meet her." Noel frowned. "Flora. Henry's wife. She called me in Baltimore and asked me to bring the jewelry. That's why I came to England." Now the words were tumbling out quickly, as if she was afraid that if she stopped, the memories would evaporate. "I had to go into D.C. and get a passport so I could leave the country. I was on the plane alone. Then they stopped me at customs—" Her head jerked up and she looked pleadingly at Jason. "But when did all *that* happen? That's not what I…remember best."

His face was stark, his posture tense as he leaned forward. "What do you remember best?"

Her voice mirrored her bewilderment. "Th-that you found out I'd been hurt. You came back and saw that I was having trouble getting back on my feet." It was amazing how much better she felt as this different version of reality poured out. "Oh, Jason, I was so glad to see you. You don't know how much that meant to me. You said it would be a good idea if we got away. Your boss lives in England. And he said he'd pay for the trip. It was so wonderful going off with you. A fresh start." By the end of the recitation, she was speaking rapidly. When she finally wound down, there was a moment of complete emptiness. For a little while, she'd felt almost normal. But once more terrible fear was rising in her chest.

"I can't stand this anymore," she whimpered, her hand flying to cover her eyes.

An instant later, Jason was beside her, pressing her face to his shoulder.

"Noel, oh, God, sweetheart, I shouldn't be doing this to you."

She held his shoulders in a death grip. "You didn't do it. I—it's in my head. The problem's in my head. Please, I want to fix it."

"I know...I know."

"I'm so frightened. I—I can't tell what's real. Is anything real?"

"Yes."

His body was an anchor, keeping her steady, keeping her moored to sanity. "You said I wouldn't believe you," she whispered. "But you have to tell me what's wrong."

Jason held her tighter. "It looks like you've got two sets of memories for the same time period. Some that include me, and some that don't. And the memories include all the emotions that go along with them."

That sounded so crazy, yet she clutched at the explanation. She knew it was right. "Yes," she whispered. The double entries were both there, like a forged set of ledgers, side by side with the real thing; the only reason she recognized the discrepancies was that Jason had forced her to audit both sets of books. She raised her head so she could meet her husband's eyes. "Two sets of memories. How? You said I'm not losing my mind."

"You're not!"

"Then how?"

"Frye has a technique for putting stuff into people's heads."

She stared at him uncomprehendingly. "But why?"

"He has reasons for wanting you to trust me."

She didn't fully understand what he was saying, yet it explained so much.

"What actually happened," he continued, "is that you came over to England alone. You were stopped at customs. They were taking you for questioning when one of Montgomery's men caught up to them."

"No!" She didn't want that to be true.

He held her gaze unwaveringly, and after a long, heavy silence, he said, "So perhaps you'd better worry about where all the warm, tender thoughts you're having about me are really coming from."

She shook her head. Her thoughts might be mixed up, but in all the uncertainty one constant had remained. Jason. Her husband. The man she loved and trusted. "Don't take that away from me."

"Noel, don't you understand?" The self-accusation in his voice tore at her heart. "I could hurt you—"

"Never."

He stood up, walking away, deliberately putting the width of the room between them. With a sweep of his hand he spoke in exasperated tones. "Noel, you keep seeing me in some sort of guardian-angel role, but I'm a lot more sinner than saint."

"It's not just memories," she countered. "It's here and now. Us. Together. Am I imagining this? The way I feel about you. The way you feel about me. I see how you keep looking at me. You want to hold me. You want to tell me everything, but you won't let yourself."

His back was to her, and she barely caught the single word he uttered. "Yes."

"Then don't torture us both because you're afraid of hurting me. It's the other way around."

He turned to face her, his eyes locking with hers. She saw the muscle jumping in his cheek. Saw the dark fire that sparked in the depth of his eyes. All at once, she felt light-headed, as if all the air had been sucked out of the room and there was nothing left to breathe.

Slowly she came up off the bed and crossed the distance between them, her arms stealing around his waist and her cheek pressing against his chest. She was half-afraid he'd pull away. When he didn't, her hands tugged at the shirttails tucked into his tight jeans until they were free and she could splay her fingers over his warm bare skin. She'd wanted to feel it for so long. Her fingers moved, and he shuddered.

Noel swallowed, her throat suddenly dry. "Just protect me from the other guys. Not you," she whispered, raising her head and brushing a kiss across his lips.

A shadow of doubt still clouded his gaze. She did her best to kiss it away.

With a primitive sound deep in his throat, he began to return the kiss, his hands moving hungrily over her neck and shoulders.

Now, she thought. Now. He can't stop now.

But he did, and a hollow place seemed to open up inside her soul.

Noel looked anxiously into Jason's eyes. His gaze was fiercely possessive—and very troubled.

Her finger traced the outline of his lips. "There's never been anyone I wanted except you."

He hauled in a ragged breath, his chest pressing against hers. "Oh, God, Noel. You think you know me, but you don't."

"You're wrong. I know everything I need to know."

"I shouldn't do this, but…sweetheart, I've wanted you forever."

Then, giving in, he took charge, kissing her with a slow yet hungry urgency that made her head spin and her body ache for more. His hands followed her curves downward to settle possessively on her hips, drawing her close to the hardness and the heat of his body. But he didn't move, and she wondered if he was giving her a chance to reconsider.

Noel fumbled with his shirt buttons. When her hands winnowed through the mat of dark hair on his chest, he let out a long sigh of pleasure. In one deft movement, he shrugged out of his shirt, baring more of his olive skin to her touch. She feathered kisses across his lean, muscled chest, until she found a long, curving scar with her lips. "You were hurt."

"I told you, I've led a dangerous life."

She tipped her head up to gaze into his eyes, yet her hands continued to move over his body. "It's part of what drew me to you. You were so tough and sure of yourself. A rebel who could make my heart pound with just a look."

His thumb stroked across her lips. "But you didn't need a guy who was always in trouble. Not when you were everything I wasn't. Respectable. Warm and kind and loving."

She nuzzled against the thumb. "You're loving."

"I want to be—with you."

"Oh, Jason—"

Her words trailed off into nothing as he skimmed his lips across her face in a string of kisses. He progressed downward to her neck, bringing a hot shiver to her skin.

"You like that," he murmured against her flesh.

"You know I do."

For a moment, he went very still. Then with a strangled sound deep in his throat, he reached for the buttons of her blouse, unfastening them one by one and then dipping into the hollow between her breasts to trace exciting little circles on her heated skin.

She felt as if a spring were tightening inside her body. After long minutes of slow torture, he slid her cotton shirt off her shoulders, unsnapped the hook on her bra and brought his hands around to cup her breasts.

As his gaze feasted on her body, her nipples hardened into taut rosy buds. In answer, his mouth covered first one, then the other with a hot sucking motion that made her insides melt.

She swayed in his embrace. With a hoarse oath, he swept her up into his arms and carried her the few feet to the bed. Bending over her, he removed the rest of her clothes. She was suddenly shy as his eager gaze took in her body. It had been so long since they'd made love that she felt almost like a bride.

But she wasn't a shy bride. She wanted this. She wanted everything. "Now you," she whispered. "I want to see you."

His eyes never left her as he removed his own clothing. For just a moment, she felt a strange sense of disorientation, as if she'd never seen him naked before. Needing the physical contact, she reached out to touch his hip, her fingers finding and tracing the jagged line of a scar. "I remember this one, too."

His eyelids squeezed shut.

"But not these." She lightly brushed the fresh bruises across his midsection and felt his stomach muscles quiver. "Do these hurt?"

He came down beside her on the bed and pulled her tightly against his taut length. "Not when I'm holding you."

When he reached to switch off the light, Noel grabbed his hand. "No, I've waited a long time to be with you like this. I want to see your face when you come inside me."

With a rough growl, he rolled her on top of himself. She pressed her face into the crinkly hair of his chest, moving her lips against his warm flesh.

"Ah, Noel."

She felt his hands as they stroked over her naked back, down her spine, across her hips. When he found the bruises she'd acquired earlier, she winced.

"You're sore."

"Just a little. From when I fell. But don't stop, please."

He was more gentle with his touch, but the tips of his fingers swept fire across her skin.

"Good. That's so good."

"God, yes."

She clung to him, savoring every touch, every sensation he could give her—storing memories that would replace the jumble in her mind. If nothing else was real, she had this night with the man she loved.

She was indeed looking up into his eyes when he entered her. He gazed down at her with a heated passion that stole her breath away. Then he was moving inside her, saying her name over and over as the tempo escalated.

Her body moved with his, quickened with his, and she felt a deep sense of homecoming along with the intensifying pleasure. She remembered this. Being with him like this. His body covering hers, moving inside hers. Trust, love, a profound sense of well-being merged as the physical sensations built.

She reached the peak, holding him tightly and calling out his name. The joy was complete when she felt him follow her over the edge into a world of pure, blinding sensation.

Chapter Nine

For long moments, Jason held Noel, kissed her, telling himself this was for her.

She knit her fingers with his as if that would keep him there beside her.

"Oh, Jason, I love you so much. I knew it would be like that again," she murmured.

He didn't say anything. There was nothing he could say.

"I wish we could lie here like this forever."

His arm tightened around her. "I love you, too."

"I thought I'd never hear you say that again. Now I know everything is going to be all right."

He wished he could agree. He couldn't get the lie past the lump in his throat. Instead, he pulled the bedclothes up around them and held her tightly, nuzzling his lips against her hair. He felt like a wanderer who had finally come home from a long, perilous journey. Home to the arms of the woman he loved.

"So tired," she whispered.

"Sleep."

"Don't let me go."

"I won't."

She settled more comfortably against him. Shortly he heard the rhythm of her breathing change.

She trusted him so completely. That burden was almost more than he could bear. Tomorrow he was going to have to pay the price for his weakness. He had no right to share her fantasy. Yet he had wanted this for so long, and he hadn't been able to deny himself her warmth or her sweet passion. And he couldn't deny himself this one last pleasure, holding her while she slept.

Long into the night, he cradled her in his arms, dreading the morning. Because when the dawn came, he was going to lose her all over again.

SHE MOANED SOMETHING in her sleep, and he was instantly alert. Perhaps she sensed the tension in his body, because her eyes blinked open.

She reached up to touch his face. "What's wrong?"

"It's early. Go back to sleep."

"Something's worrying you. Let me help."

He didn't want it to end. But reality had returned with the cold light of morning. He inched away from Noel so that he could meet her eyes.

"How are you feeling?"

She considered the answer for several seconds. "Better."

"Good. Because if you're not going back to sleep, we have to talk."

He saw the denial in her eyes and plowed on. "There are a couple of big problems we put on hold last night. Like your double set of memories."

He saw her lower lip tremble. For a moment the thought of hurting her more—no, losing her—paralyzed his muscles. Then he pulled the covers away from his naked body.

"What are you doing?" She stared at him, shivering in the cool air as her eyes traveled from the broad expanse of his chest downward to his narrow waist and then farther still. He felt the stirrings of desire again but tried to ignore them. With fingers that weren't entirely steady, he took her hand and flattened it over the jagged scar that marred his hip.

Her fingers moved against his flesh.

He forced himself to do what he had to do. "You said you remembered this scar."

"Yes."

"You saw it on our honeymoon five years ago."

"I remembered your body." She hesitated, as if she wasn't quite sure it was true. "What point are you trying to make?"

"How did I say I got hurt?"

She looked at him blankly, then began to speak in the jerky voice he'd come to recognize. The voice that gave away the false data being played back. "In the marines. In South America. You couldn't tell me what country, because it was a secret operation."

"Noel, I didn't have this scar five years ago. I got it when Frye sent me to Eastern Europe to smuggle out the names of former Communist agents. A couple of forcibly retired East German SSD men tried their damnedest to stop me."

He watched her face as she struggled to take in what he was saying.

"But...I saw...I...remember—"

"It's like the memories from the past thirty-six hours. You *think* you remember," he said as gently as he could.

She buried her face in her hands. "Are you talking about our honeymoon, the Caribbean, that night we danced on the patio—are you trying to say it didn't...?"

She trailed off, then began again as something else surfaced. "Before we left. There was a little Greek restaurant. In Baltimore. Your cousin owns it. We went to tell him we were getting married, and he was so happy about it. He gave us dinner, and after the place closed, there was a pretty wild celebration." A smile flickered on her lips. "They introduced me to an old Greek custom—smashing drinking glasses on the floor to show you're happy. You were throwing them down. And your uncle was sweeping them into the corner. And everybody was dancing, together in a circle. I didn't know the steps, but you taught me."

He stared at her in disbelief. "You...that's one of your memories?"

"How could I forget it?"

He swallowed painfully. "Noel, I'm sorry. You don't know how much I wish it were all true. But five years ago I was in Honduras—not Baltimore."

Noel sat up and covered her ears, as if she were trying to hold together a fragile mosaic assembled in her head. Jason came up beside her, reached over and pulled her hands down to rest on his shoulders.

"Stop it. Why are you doing this to me?"

"To save your life." He lifted her chin so that she was forced to look at him. "Noel, listen to me. You're clinging to a set of false recollections because that's part of what Sir Douglas wants you to do."

"No." She tried to twist away.

"You have to listen." He took her by the shoulders. "Sir Douglas calls himself the Sovereign because he's more powerful than the ruler of any country. And he's absolutely ruthless. He makes his living buying and stealing information. Sometimes he sells it back to the original owner. Sometimes he uses it for blackmail. Other times he auctions it off to the highest bidder. Or when it suits his purposes, he simply delivers it into the hands that will do him the most good. Your uncle was one of his couriers. He carried information around the world concealed in pieces of antique jewelry.''

Noel stared at him, her head swimming. Uncle Henry. And Jason. "*You* work for him," she breathed.

"When you're dishonorably discharged from the marines, you don't have a lot of job offers."

"You're telling me you work for a criminal." The words came out slowly, against her will. Merely saying them set up a pounding in her skull.

He winced. "I work for a man who was willing to take me in when the U.S. government made damn sure I wasn't going to get a job with anyone else."

Silence filled the little room. Despite the pain and the fear and the lingering confusion in her mind, she struggled to hold on to the truth. Jason had said she didn't know him. She hadn't dreamed the extent of her ignorance or naiveté.

He was watching her face intently. "Do you understand?" he asked.

She nodded, not trusting herself to speak.

"So now that we've gotten through the preliminaries, we can get to the really bad part," he said in a flat voice.

"I thought that was the bad part."

"It's not as bad as Sir Douglas's private research lab in Switzerland—where a group of warped scientists is carrying out mind-control experiments."

Noel felt as if someone had thrown open the window, letting a chill breeze into the room.

Jason went on. "They started working with dogs, implanting electrodes in their heads to control their actions. Then they moved on to primates. I'm not sure if

they had any human guinea pigs in the early stages.
Maybe Frye was waiting for a less invasive procedure. But
I do know the experimenters turned their attention to
memory because they decided that might be the key to
control.''

"What are you trying to tell me?'' Noel whispered
hoarsely.

"I've been racking my brain trying to piece together
everything I can about those damn experiments. And I
hate to have to say this, but—'' He hesitated, swiping the
dark hair back from his forehead. "Sweetheart, I think
Sir Douglas had someone put an implant in your head.''

In the face of her mute horror, Jason drew in a ragged
breath. "Maybe at first he was only using it to confuse
your thoughts—or make you feel compelled to take this
trip to England. Now I'm pretty sure it's sending false
information to your brain.''

Noel felt as if someone had slapped a fistful of ice
against the back of her neck. A shiver raced down her
spine, the cold seeping into her bones.

"No!''

Jason's hands soothed over her shoulders, but the
contact brought no comfort. "Oh, Noel, I wish it weren't
true. I wish I didn't have to make you believe it. Remember when I found you huddled on the floor upstairs
in Frye's cottage? It was after you saw the fake passport.''

"It's *not* a fake,'' Noel insisted, desperation coloring
her voice.

The look Jason gave her was filled with apology. "Yes,
it is. And you knew it. You knew it, and you were trying
to run away because you didn't trust me. Then everything changed and you suddenly 'remembered' we were
married.''

Noel's lips moved, but no words came out. Slowly, almost against her own will, she traced the raised line of the scar at the back of her head. She'd done that before. As if she'd somehow known all the mental disturbances, all the confusion was coming from that spot.

"God . . . *no*." The protest welled up from deep in her soul.

Her mind. Her thoughts. What was hers? What was someone else's invention?

A wave of helpless terror coursed through her, and she began to shake uncontrollably. Jason took her back in his arms, sliding down under the covers with her, pressing her body against his, giving her his warmth.

"No. Oh, please, no."

"Noel, sweetheart, I think there's something we can do about it."

She realized suddenly that he'd said the words more than once. "What?" she whispered.

"I'm hoping I can take it out."

"Oh, Jason, thank God." The relief was overwhelming.

"It could be dangerous."

"Why?"

"Because I'm not a doctor. And I wish I knew more about the damn device. I'm making assumptions. I'm guessing it's just under your skin because that would be the easiest thing to do. But what if I'm wrong?"

Her hands dug into his forearms. "Please, just get it out of me!"

She heard him swallow. "When I do, you're not going to feel the same way about me."

"Yes, I will."

"The good memories will be gone." His voice was gritty with pain—and regret.

"No," she protested. "No, they won't be."

He was silent a moment before saying, "I wish I believed that." He took her face in his hands, looking at her as if he was memorizing her features. She stared at him just as intently. They hugged tightly. Then he eased out of the bed.

As she watched him walk naked across the room and reach for his duffel bag, the full impact of what he proposed to do hit her. Was he right? Would all these wonderful feelings of warmth and love for him be gone?

Making love with him had seemed so right . . . so familiar. She didn't want to discover they had never made love before. That they weren't married. Yet now the other memories, the ones she supposed were real, hovered like a cold, gaping darkness. As it opened up before her, Noel shrank away. She wanted her mind back again, but she was suddenly terrified to pay the price.

"Jason!"

He turned back toward her, and the look in his eyes was a mirror of her own anguish.

"You can't . . ." She swallowed hard. "You can't take it *all* away from me. Please. I want to remember last night."

His look softened. "What I'm hoping is that you *will* remember it. Because it may be all I have left to bring you back to me."

"It will," she vowed, at the same time wondering how she could be certain of anything.

Noel grabbed a handful of clothing from her luggage and vanished into the bathroom. Getting dressed made her feel a little less vulnerable. But not much.

She wasn't sure what she'd expected when she emerged. But it wasn't Jason sitting in an easy chair with a tape recorder on the table.

"What's that for?" she asked.

"Both our lives may depend on your being able to act like you're still under control. After I remove the implant, the tape may be the only way we'll have of *remembering* what you're supposed to believe with it in your head."

Noel shuddered but sat down at the table.

For the next forty-five minutes, Jason prodded her memory, and Noel did her best to cooperate, battling confusion as scenes clashed with each other. She sat with her hands clenching painfully in her lap, as if that could hold her together. Sometimes pictures and feelings popped into her head. Sometimes she had to ignore the throbbing in her brain and dig for answers. Always, she watched Jason's face for clues to what was true and what was false. Unfortunately, he held his reactions under iron control, and she learned nothing.

Finally Jason sighed. "I've been stalling for the last fifteen minutes."

"Why?"

"Because every decision we make is dangerous. What if I'm wrong about this, and I screw up your mind? *Permanently.*"

"That's a chance I'm prepared to take, because I *can't* stay like this. So, please, let's get on with it."

He stood up and got a small leather case out of his duffel bag. When he opened it, she saw the contents went beyond a mere first-aid kit.

"I can handle a bunch of emergencies," he said. "But I don't have any topical anesthetic."

Her eyes flicked to the bed. "I guess I ought to lie down."

Before she could turn away, he folded her into his arms, simply holding her for several moments and then covering her mouth with his in a kiss that was equal parts desperation and passion. She clung to him, kissing him back with all the love she felt, wishing that he never had to let go.

When he started to ease away, she murmured a protest.

Tenderly he kissed her closed eyelids, her eyebrows, her cheeks. She looked down so that he wouldn't see the moisture in her eyes, and his lips moved against her hair. "Noel, sweetheart, try to remember that I love you."

She felt her heart turn over. He'd kissed her, held her, even said those words before. But hearing him say them now meant everything to her. She was so choked with emotion that her reply was a ghost of a whisper. "Oh, Jason, there's not a chance that I'll forget."

She knew he had heard by the way he caressed her. She leaned against him, absorbing his strength—his essence. But finally she knew it was time.

Trying to move briskly, Noel turned to the bed, removed the pillows, straightened the covers and spread a clean towel on the quilt before lying down. She cradled her head on her hands and closed her eyes. When she felt his fingers brush aside her hair, she tensed.

She smelled the stringent odor of antiseptic and braced herself for the pain.

"Are you ready? I'm going to do it now."

"I'm ready."

The pain she felt was more than a physical sensation. It was like a needle jabbing and tearing at the essence of her being. Of Noel Zacharias. Noel Emery.

Memories flashed and collided. Overlapping and blurring, new ones replacing old, like slides shoved haphazardly into a projector. Good and bad. Sweet and painful.

A sob welled in her throat as she looked down into her mother's grave.

Then she smiled as she spied Jason lying naked on a wide bed. At the cabin in the woods. He smiled back and held out his arms.

He vanished, replaced by the killer in Mr. Dubinski's grocery store. No. It was the other man. The one she'd worked for. The one who'd thrown her to the sofa in his office and— Turning, she tried to run and became tangled in the light streaming through the stained-glass window over the door at 43 Light Street.

Her fingernails dug into the skin of her forearms, but she didn't feel that pain. She was somewhere else. Other places. Other times. Swamped by a rising tide of overlapping feelings, sensations...memories. They came faster, sharper. Until there was nothing left but pure emotions. Need. Desire. Fear. Love. Hate. A terrible sense of loss.

From somewhere far away, Jason called to her, but it was too late.

She was being ripped in two—torn to pieces by a shattering explosion. She screamed as the universe turned to fire.

Chapter Ten

The scalpel dropped to the floor with a clatter that barely registered above the screams that filled the bedroom.

"Noel. Oh, God, Noel. What have I done to you?"

Jason grasped Noel's shoulders, turning her over so he could see her face. For a moment she stared at him in terror, then her gaze went hazy and unfocused as if she wasn't seeing him at all.

At the same time, she started beating with her fists at his shoulders and trying to tear herself from his grasp.

"No. Get away from me. I won't let you do it." The words were blurred, indistinct. But he heard.

"Noel. It's Jason. I won't hurt you," he said over and over, fighting the sick feeling that taking out the chip had been the worst thing he could do to her.

The small fists continued to pound. Her breath came in frantic puffs.

"Gilmore." The name tore from her throat.

Jason felt his insides twist, and his hands tightened convulsively on her shoulders. Sir Douglas had told him that name. Had told him what he thought a man named Gilmore had done to Noel. When she'd been living alone in Baltimore.

Oh, God, it was true.

Her nails raked his arms. The pain was his punishment, but it was nothing compared to what she had endured. As gently as he could, he forced her to stay with him on the mattress.

"You're not going to—no—"

Again he said his name. And hers, wondering if there was any way to get through to her. "Sweetheart, I'm trying to help you."

The change was abrupt. Suddenly she went slack except for her ragged breathing. Her eyes blinked, looking up at him in confusion. When she began to cry softly, the sound cut all the way to his soul. He stroked her cheek.

She looked as if she was struggling very hard to get control of herself. Gradually the tears stopped, and her breathing slowed. He handed her a tissue, and she wiped her eyes.

"Do you know where we are?"

"In . . . England."

"Do you remember what happened this morning?"

"The . . . chip. You told me about the chip."

"I took it out."

"Thank God."

When he had restitched the incision, he picked up a square of gauze from the table. "Here's what I took out of you." It was a wafer-thin piece of silicon about one-fourth-inch wide and a half-inch long.

Noel raised her head to stare at it, as if she couldn't believe something so small and insignificant looking could have done so much damage.

"How do you feel?"

"Empty. No. Half-full. Like half of me's gone," she said in a small voice. "The best part."

"No. The best part of you is all there."

She looked as if she didn't believe him. "Don't give me easy reassurances."

"Sweetheart, I'm so sorry."

"Don't call me that. You don't have to pretend anymore."

"Noel—"

"I remember our talk this morning. And what happened last night." A flush spread across her cheeks. "You tried to tell me the chip was controlling my memories and my emotions. But I didn't believe you. I've been reliving a marriage that didn't happen."

Jason felt as if the words had flayed his flesh. He wanted to grab her, hold her, tell her the feelings they had for each other went a lot further than the cursed implant. But he couldn't bear the look of pain and humiliation in her eyes, so he took a long time carefully wrapping the device he'd removed from her scalp. Then he carried the scalpel into the bathroom and began to wash it.

When he came back, Noel's eyelids were closed. He stood looking at her, taking in the dark lashes lying softly against her cheeks. The bloodless pallor of her skin. The vulnerable curve of her lips. Last night those lips had eagerly sought his. Now she probably wished he'd vanish with the memories.

At first he assumed she was simply shutting him out—running away in the only way she could. Then he saw from the even rise and fall of her chest that she was asleep.

He hoped she'd feel better when she woke—physically and mentally. There was no reason to think she'd feel any differently about him.

NOEL WAS DRIFTING, dreaming. Warm, lazy dreams. About the cabin beside the lake. Jason had caught a striped bass for dinner, and she had picked a bowl of wild blueberries.

Only somehow the fish and blueberries had disappeared, and they were sitting in front of bowls of pea soup. But neither one of them was hungry.

Her eyes blinked open.

Her husband was sitting in a chair beside the bed, watching her. She started to hold out her arms. Then reality returned with a sharp stab, and her hands dropped back to her sides. Jason Zacharias wasn't her husband. She should have listened when he tried to tell her that.

"How do you feel?"

Mortified. Frightened. Confused. "Hungry."

"That's probably a good sign. I can make you some tea. And there are biscuits."

Jason had the electric kettle on the bureau quickly boiling. As Noel watched him empty a packet of sugar and a small container of milk into her cup, she wondered how he knew what she liked in her tea. Then she decided that he'd probably been briefed on that, along with everything else.

He waited while she sat up and took the cup.

"I need to find out what you remember."

The words called up pictures and sensations—swirling in her head. Some of them were real and some were false. She gripped the saucer as she recalled how she'd practically begged Jason to make love to her. When she'd thought he was her husband. He wasn't. He was little more than a stranger, and all the warm, loving emotions she'd felt for him had come from a chip in her head.

The chip was gone. Yet wisps of love still clung to her mind like ground mist before the sun could burn it off.

Being married to Jason had seemed so right. So real. Even though she understood that was all an illusion, it still *felt* as if she were married to this man. No, it was worse than that. She still *wanted* to be married to him. Noel stroked her hand across the covers, smoothing out the wrinkles and wishing it were that easy to brush away her emotional confusion—and her embarrassment at being so dependent on a man she hardly knew.

"Can you tell me when you first saw me in England?"

The businesslike tone of his voice was a relief—at least he was trying to make this easier for her. "You rescued me from one of Montgomery's men."

"What happened after that?"

Noel told him about coming to the cottage. And finding the passport. When she got to that part, she stopped, going numb all over as she raised her hand toward the back of her head and then stopped abruptly before she reached the new wound. "It hurt."

He leaned toward her. "Your wound?"

"No. Inside my head. Just as I was climbing out the window, I—I was paralyzed by a terrible pain, like lava rushing through my brain cells."

Jason swore.

"That must have been when your friend Sir Douglas switched on the memory generator."

"Yes."

They stared at each other silently.

"Do you recall a honeymoon—"

"—in the Caribbean," she finished the sentence for him.

He looked as if he was going to ask another question. But he closed his lips, and Noel felt a sense of loss she didn't want to examine too closely. Instead, she tried to describe the way the manufactured memory played in her mind.

"It's like remembering a movie I saw." A terrible feeling of emptiness hit her then, and she tried to stifle a broken little sob.

His hand came out toward her. He touched her briefly and withdrew. "I'm sorry."

She wasn't sure what she was seeing in his eyes; she only knew that if she kept staring into them, she'd come undone.

"After my uncle was shot. You took me away and pumped me for information," she said to fill the silence and then stopped short, her face taking on a look that was a mixture of incredulity and horror. "My God. And the shooting. I—I remember everything right up to the shooting."

"That's good."

"Is it?"

Before she could get lost in the remembered sorrow, he stood up. "Come on. You need to get out of here for a while. Get ready, and we'll find a pub."

"Is that safe?"

"It should be, since Montgomery will assume we didn't stick around here."

Noel was surprised to find it was late afternoon when they emerged from their cottage.

"I paid for an extra day while you were asleep," Jason explained. "We don't have to leave until tomorrow."

Noel took a deep breath of the fresh country air. "I didn't know how much I needed to get out of that room," she said softly.

"You needed a break."

It was a short ride to the village pub—the Boar's Head.

Noel stared at the brass letters riveted to the side of the stone building. They said Courage.

"'Courage,'" she read aloud, marveling at the aptness.

"A brand of ale," Jason explained. "The company owns the pub."

Even though he'd said it was safe, he had her wait in the car until he'd gone in and had a look around. Then he came and got her.

They ate jacket potatoes—hers with cheddar cheese and his with baked beans. He ordered ginger beer for her and ale for himself.

Once or twice during the meal, they both looked up at the same time. As their eyes met, Noel would feel a little rush of pleasure. Then she'd remember what was real and what wasn't and look quickly down at her food.

Why were the feelings still there? Even when she knew they were manufactured in a Swiss lab? Apparently it was going to take awhile to convince herself that there was no true bond between herself and Jason.

"Now that you've had some time to adjust, do you think you can tell the difference between what's real and what isn't?" Jason asked after they'd driven back to the cottage once again.

Noel swallowed, wishing the question weren't so close to what she'd been thinking earlier. "I hope so."

"Let's try." He began to call up a rapid series of scenes. After each one, he asked if it had happened.

She did her best to cooperate. Usually an answer came to her immediately. Occasionally an image she knew was false was so appealing that she had to clench her fists to drive it out of her mind.

She breathed a sigh of relief when Jason finally called a halt. "Do I have it right?"

"As far as I can tell."

Noel sighed deeply, feeling a small bit of the tension ease out of her shoulders.

"Do you remember saving me from Montgomery's men?" he asked suddenly.

"Yes." Her hands curled inward as if feeling again the cold metal of the machine gun. Again she saw a man whirl toward her. Bright splotches of red appeared on his shirt as he slid to the floor. Her hands flattened against her face. "Oh, Lord. I killed him."

"To save me," Jason said in a low voice.

She saw him take in a deep draft of air and let it out slowly. "Noel, I'm going to tell you some things that put my life in your hands just as effectively as if you were still holding a loaded gun."

Her head jerked up.

"I'm in the middle of a very dangerous game. I couldn't tell you anything about it before because of the chip in your head. Sir Douglas is planning to question you. With the controller in place, all he'd have to do was press the right button to get you to play back everything I've told you."

She'd been concentrating on trying to feel normal. Now he was forcing her to confront the rest of her problems. "Jason, this morning you told me I didn't know you. Now you're telling me you're still taking me to Sir Douglas Frye?"

"Yes."

"Why? Why should I agree to go there with you?"

With a low curse, he sprang across the space that separated them, and grabbed her by the forearms. "Sir Douglas Frye is a cold-blooded killer who will do anything for money. And I mean anything. Start civil wars. Provide the know-how for biological and chemical weapons. If it's profitable, he does it. He's been consolidating his power for the past twenty years. But now I'm going to put him out of business.''

Noel wanted to believe him. Still she knew how dangerous it was to simply swallow his explanation whole. ''But you work for him.''

''He *thinks* I'm grateful that he gave me a job. He *thinks* I'm loyal to him. He *thinks* I like the money and power I've earned in his employ. I've spent almost four years of my life laying that groundwork and gaining his trust.''

She tried to absorb everything he was saying. ''You're taking some big risks going against him.''

''It was my choice. I volunteered for the assignment. And the U.S. government is paying me a very large sum of money to do it.''

''Didn't you tell me the U.S. government was out to make sure you couldn't get another job?''

He nodded. ''It's true. But it was planned that way. I was busted for dealing drugs to recruits at Camp Lejeune and spent a couple of months in the stockade. According to the scenario we worked out, none of the buyers would testify, so I got off with a dishonorable discharge. But it was all staged—all part of the plan to make Frye confident he was recruiting a ruthless, bitter man, and that he had something to hold over me.''

''Are you saying this . . . scheme has been in the works for years?''

''Yeah. It's that kind of operation. Like when the Russians used to put agents in a country and let them work up to a position of authority—doing nothing until they got the signal to act. Frye's information sources are so extensive he wouldn't have fallen for anything superficial.''

She sat in stunned silence, trying to imagine what his life must have been like over the past few years. Then, carefully, she said, "That's an awful lot to swallow."

"I'm hoping it makes you understand how carefully this whole thing has been set up. And if you want a character reference for Frye, think about what he did to you," he continued. "And your uncle. He kept Henry Marconi in virtual bondage for years. Didn't you think it was strange the way your uncle used to disappear for weeks at a time? Didn't you wonder why he never got close to anyone?"

Noel had always felt that there was some painful secret hidden by Uncle Henry's jovial exterior. "What about Flora?"

"The Sovereign's invention. You don't remember your uncle ever mentioning her before, do you?"

"No. Mom had told me he'd been stationed in England in the fifties. That's why Flora's story seemed to fit. But Uncle Henry never volunteered any information about his past, and the few times I asked, he made it clear that there were parts of his life he didn't want to discuss."

"Noel, right now, I can't prove every detail I've told you—although my trial is a matter of public record. What you need to understand is that you've gotten yourself caught in the middle of a very elaborate plan to put Frye out of business. I'm damn sorry you're involved. But it's too late to call it off, even if I could. If it gets cocked up now, a lot of people are going to die."

She stared at him, unable to respond.

"I'm sorry. I'm pushing you too fast." He stood quickly. "You'd better get some sleep, and we'll talk later."

"What are you going to do?"

"Think about how to get us out of this alive."

HE CURSED HIMSELF for giving her too much to deal with all at once, when she was still coping with the after-effects of the chip. But now that he'd told her about Frye, he desperately needed her cooperation if he was going to pull off this operation. The other things he needed from her, the more personal things—well, there was hardly a chance that she'd give him any of those. But he had had a day with her—and a night.

Long after Noel had fallen asleep, he sat in the arm-chair staring at her face, sifting back over every detail of the time when she'd thought she was married to him, re-membering her warm little glances, her gestures, her loving words. He'd craved that from her more than he'd wanted to admit. Craved it enough to make the mistake of letting her seduce him.

But at least he had something to be grateful for. Noel's mind was mending.

He'd already considered and discarded alternate plans. She'd be in more danger on her own. From Frye, for starters.

He shuddered, thinking of things he'd seen the Sover-eign do. If he didn't take Sir Douglas out now, Noel would never be safe. The man was capable of tracking her to the ends of the earth to make an example of her.

And in the short run, there was Montgomery. And the British authorities. At this point, they might well shoot first and ask questions later.

There was only one way the two of them were going to work their way out of this cursed situation. He had to play the hand he'd been dealt. And he had to hope he was a better poker player than Sir Douglas Frye.

Carefully, in calculated, detailed terms, his mind devised and rejected a half-dozen ways to stack the deck in his favor. Then he realized there was something he hadn't considered. The chip he'd taken out of Noel's head.

After retrieving the little package, he slowly unwound the gauze and stared at the implant. Then he picked up the innocent-looking rectangle in a pair of tweezers and held it to the light, examining the network of fine lines etched into the silicon.

Pulling a powerful magnifying device from its case, he took a better look.

As he followed the well-defined paths, his gaze worked its way to the edges of the implant. There was something in the right-hand corner that he would have missed altogether without the light and the powerful magnification.

His body went rigid, and the breath solidified in his lungs as he looked from the chip to the sleeping woman in the bed.

NOEL OPENED HER EYES and saw Jason sprawled in one of the armchairs, his dark hair tousled, his shirt wrinkled. He was asleep, his long legs crossed at the ankles and stretched to their full length, his back at what looked like an uncomfortable angle. An image of another time he'd fallen asleep in a chair leaped into her mind. On their honeymoon. He'd gotten a phone call. He'd been worried about—

Her mind came up against a blank wall.

He'd been worried about—

The memory flitted away, leaving her alone with the man. Her gaze probed his features. They were taut with fatigue and strain that sleep hadn't erased.

Why wasn't he in bed with her, she wondered with a rush of warmth and concern. Anxious to take him in her arms, she shifted toward him. The bed creaked. His eyes snapped open, and his gaze locked with hers—burned into hers.

In that blinding second, she remembered what her conscious mind had blotted out. Half-asleep, she'd been confused. No longer.

He grimaced as he straightened, his eyes going to the closed blinds where a strip of watery sunlight filtered into the room, and then back to her. "How do you feel this morning?"

"Better."

"Good. I wish—" He stopped abruptly and swiped back the dark hair that had fallen across his forehead.

"What were you going to say?"

"I should have let my brain catch up with my mouth. I was going to say I wish we had some way of knowing whether you're completely back to normal."

His uncertainty brought a tingle of fear. Last night, she'd started to believe she had come out of it in one piece. But how long was she going to have to question every thought she had? She covered her disquiet by standing up, striding toward her luggage and looking for something to wear. After pulling out a pair of jeans and a knit shirt, she took a deep breath and straightened. "So what's next?"

"Let me have a look at the incision."

Noel stood very still as he came toward her. Dipping her head, she waited for his touch. It was very gentle as he pushed her hair aside and examined her scalp.

"Well?" she managed.

"It looks good."

His fingers moved against her scalp in a gesture that would have been a caress—under other circumstances. For just a moment Noel rested her forehead against his chest. Then she pushed herself away. It didn't make sense that she should want to be close to him, that she should crave the comfort that gave her.

They both turned back to the business of getting ready. As she searched for her toilet articles, Noel's fingers brushed the jewelry bag she was supposed to have delivered to Flora. My God. She'd almost forgotten.

With jerky movements, she opened the zipper and shook a brooch, a locket and a wide bracelet into her hand. They were all overblown nineteenth-century pieces, although each was very different in character. The bracelet was fashioned from one curved piece of silver, circled with a raised design of repoussé work. The brooch was shaped like a Nile lily and studded with lapis. The locket had an oval door that swung open on recessed hinges. Noel had examined and put a value on each piece before she'd left Baltimore. However, she hadn't seen anything unusual about any of them.

She knew Jason was watching her even before she looked up. "Okay, so I was sent here to smuggle some sort of secret information into England. What is it? And which one of these has a secret compartment?"

"All of them have secret compartments," Jason informed her. "Your uncle supplied some of the Sovereign's most valuable dispatch cases, and Sir Douglas was anxious to make sure he got them back so he could keep on using them."

"But that's not the main point, is it?" Noel persisted. "One of these little beauties is stuffed full of illegal documents that Frye's waiting for. And Montgomery wants. And the customs service thinks I have. Who am I betraying? The U.S. government? A private corporation?"

Jason tossed the shirt he was holding onto the end of the bed and crossed the room. He gave Noel a long look before taking the bracelet out of her hand. When he pressed his fingers across the face of a daisy, it slid aside, revealing a small compartment.

Noel reached inside and plucked out a tiny, folded sheet of paper. "What is it?"

Jason's features were grim. "A fake."

Chapter Eleven

Noel looked from him to the folded paper. "I—I don't understand."

"The real information was on the chip."

With a horrible feeling of disbelief, Noel sat down heavily on the end of the bed.

"I had a good look at it after you went to sleep. The Swiss lab supplied the circuitry. Someone else added a microdot."

"A microdot?" Noel struggled to understand.

"Yes. They're used to compress hundreds of words to less than a millimeter. Like the old saw about the Twenty-Third Psalm engraved on the head of a pin. Frye was using you as a courier, all right. The jewelry was simply a nice bonus."

"He *told* you?"

"Of course not! I figured it out last night. Now we know why Sir Douglas was so anxious to get you to Castle Lockwood. Which means it's going to be damn hard to convince him that he doesn't want you there tomorrow."

The jewelry tumbled from Noel's numb hand onto the rug. Jason stooped to pick it up and replaced the tiny sheet of paper in the bracelet. He continued to speak, almost to himself. "If Frye sees the fresh incision, he's going to know I've double-crossed him. Unfortunately, after considering all the angles, the best delaying tactic I can think of is to get the thugs who tried to kill me to come after us again."

"That's insane."

"Exactly. I'd be a lunatic to set us up for something like that. Which is why the Sovereign just might buy it. Also, he wouldn't want us to lead them straight to the castle. If they attacked the place, it might upset his big plans."

Noel was trying to come to grips with that information when Jason knelt again and began to dig in his luggage. "You'd better put this on."

"What?"

He held out his hand. In it was a gleaming yellow band. A wedding ring.

Noel's breath caught as she stared down at the circle of gold. A wedding band. It symbolized so much. Yet in this case, it symbolized nothing.

"It goes with the passport. The customs service isn't looking for Mrs. Jason Zacharias." Without waiting for an answer, Jason grabbed her hand, thrust the ring into it and brushed past her into the bathroom. Noel's fingers closed around the metal circle. It was warm from Jason's touch.

For a moment, she couldn't see though the blur of tears in her eyes. The old phrase, "better to have loved and lost than never to have loved at all" stole into her mind.

In this case, it wasn't true. Still, there was something compelling about the ring clutched in her fist. Opening her hand, she stared at it again. With a little gulp, she slipped it on. It was the correct size. And it felt achingly right circling her flesh.

What kind of ring had he given her before they'd gone on their honeymoon?

Noel shook her head in denial. What a question. There had been no honeymoon and no ring. But apparently she still couldn't stop the memories of what might have been from ambushing her when her guard was down.

She sank to the edge of the bed, pressing her fist against her mouth to keep from moaning. No matter how many times she told herself the emotions were counterfeit, she couldn't let go of the feeling that she loved Jason.

THEY LEFT Still Water Farm forty-five minutes later, after a big English breakfast in the farm dining room. At least, Jason had eaten eggs and bacon. Noel had barely gotten through the toast and cereal. Jason had asked their hostess which area sights they should visit and had thanked her for recommending Bath and Stonehenge. But when he'd reached the main road, he turned in the other direction.

She sensed his tension as he drove.

"What's wrong?"

"I have to check in with Frye. He's going to want to know why I didn't do it yesterday."

"What are you going to tell him?"

"That you were sick. I'm going to make it sound as if you were having some sort of reaction to the chip."

She felt her chest tighten. "Will he believe that?"

"I'll make it convincing."

He pulled into the parking lot of a pub along the highway and walked to an outdoor phone booth partly screened by a neatly trimmed hedgerow.

As Noel watched him pick up the receiver and dial, she felt every muscle in her body clench. He was getting new instructions from the master criminal, the Sovereign.

Since she couldn't hear the conversation, she concentrated on Jason's body language. Sometimes he stood up straight and spoke rapidly. Sometimes his shoulders hunched as he gripped the receiver. Sometimes he looked as though he was vigorously arguing an important point.

She saw him take a deep breath as he ended the call, and she realized she was imitating the gesture. He didn't say anything as he climbed back into the driver's seat.

"What's wrong?"

Jason slid his hands along the circle of the steering wheel but said nothing.

"Jason?"

"Sir Douglas wanted to know if I'd gotten a chance to enjoy your wifely charms before you took ill."

"And?"

"I told him I had—because we've got to stick as close to the truth as we can."

Her cheeks heated.

"I didn't like talking about you." He turned to her. "But I had to give him what he expected from the Jason Zacharias he thinks he knows." He sucked a long breath and let it out slowly. "From the moment I took that chip out, I committed myself to walking a tightrope."

Noel closed her eyes, thinking about the terrible confusion in her mind. The inability to trust her own thoughts. The feeling that she'd lost control. Only remnants were left. "I didn't thank you for taking it out," she whispered.

He leaned toward her, gathering her into his arms. She laid her head against his shoulder, feeling comforted by his embrace. If only—

She stopped herself before she could finish the thought.

"You had a lot to deal with," he murmured.

"So did you."

For long moments, neither of them moved. She longed to ask him what he was feeling, but she didn't dare.

Then Jason straightened. "He wants us at Castle Lockwood next Thursday."

Noel's hand rose toward the back of her head. She stopped herself before she touched the new stitches. "That—that's only a week. Is it long enough?"

He chose to answer only part of the question. "If the incision's not healed, you can tell him it got infected."

Jason started the engine and pulled back onto the narrow road.

"Where are we going now?"

"We're going to play a game of hopscotch."

"With Sir Douglas?"

"No. With Montgomery's men. They've got to think we're out in the cold and trying to evade them."

"Out in the cold," Noel repeated.

"And we *do* have to make sure they don't find us. Until we pick the time and the place."

"Will they think we're going right to Scotland?"

"Yes. They'll assume we're speeding north. So we'll stick around here."

They ended up driving less than fifty miles along country roads, stopping at an even more isolated farm with guest cottages. This time, Noel noted with relief, the little room had double beds.

Jason picked up ham, cheese and pickle sandwiches at a pub in the tiny nearby village, and they ate at a small table beside a window that looked out over rolling fields that swept away toward low hills. Nearby, cows grazed peacefully.

After wadding up the sandwich wrappers and tossing them into the trash, Jason opened his duffel bag and got out the tape recorder.

"We've bought ourselves a week to get ready. Let's get to work."

It seemed like an impossible setting for plotting the overthrow of an international master criminal. "Are you going to tell me about Sir Douglas's organization?" Noel asked.

"No. It's safer if we stick with what was on the chip."

She squeezed her hands together under the table and nodded.

Jason rewound the tape and began to play it. His voice came first. "What do you remember about my coming back to Baltimore?"

Her taped voice answered. "I was in trouble. You knew I needed you, so you came to help me."

Noel felt the sandwich congeal in her stomach as she listened to the recitation. It was her. But it wasn't. There was a little hesitation before she began to talk. And then an odd, dreamy quality to the way she spoke.

"What do you remember about the shooting in your uncle's shop?"

The same pause before she began to speak again. After a moment, she reached out and pressed the Off button. "I sound drugged."

"I know hearing yourself sound like that is upsetting, but it wasn't you. It wasn't your fault."

"I can't imitate that."

"You don't have to. He'll assume that after a week absorbing them, the memories will come more naturally."

She nodded. That wasn't the only thing bothering her. How could she talk to Jason about the way she'd acted when she thought she was in love with him?

He was silent for several seconds, and she wondered if he knew what she was thinking. "You're going to have to listen to the whole tape," he said gently. "But not now. Why don't we try something else. Let's make sure we both know the chronology of what Sir Douglas wants you to think happened. Tell it to me in your own words."

That was hardly any easier. Noel took a deep breath. "We were supposed to have gotten married five years ago and gone on a honeymoon in the Caribbean. You left me in Baltimore because you had a dangerous assignment. After that I went out and found a job with Laura Roswell."

She wasn't able to keep her gaze from flicking to his face. His dark eyes had turned liquid with what looked like anguish. When he realized she was looking at him, he got up and turned quickly away. None of what she'd recounted had really happened. Yet he seemed as disturbed by the recitation as she.

"And the rest of it?" he said, without turning away from the window.

"The part in the middle is pretty much the way it happened. I guess Sir Douglas figured he didn't have to fiddle with that. Then you came back to comfort me after my uncle died. The details of the trip over here are a bit fuzzy—as if the scriptwriter figured it wasn't important—or didn't have time to put them in. After you got me away from Montgomery's man, our memories should be the same."

He was standing with his hands clenched at his sides. She looked at his stiff arms and rigid shoulders, wanting to get up and knead the tightness out of his muscles. A wife would do that. But Jason Zacharias didn't have a wife.

A sudden image of how it had been making love with him bloomed in her mind, and she was very glad he was standing with his back to her. He had been sweet. And tender. And passionate. And he had made it very good for her. Given her everything she would have wanted from the husband who had finally come back to her.

Neither one of them spoke. Finally Noel found her voice.

"You're upset."

"Worried," he corrected.

She didn't challenge him on that. "About what?"

"Yesterday, all I could think about was getting that damn mind-control device out of your head. I'm just now realizing how hard it's going to be to pull this whole stunt off."

"Then why are we doing it? What would happen if you showed up at Castle Lockwood without me?"

"I can't go back without you."

Noel took a deep breath and let it out slowly. She'd been with this man less than two days, yet her knowledge of him was beginning to feel instinctive. "Jason, what is it you haven't told me? Why is getting Sir Douglas so important to you?"

A charged moment of silence passed as Jason turned to face her. "All right. You want the whole truth? He killed my best friend. Ray Donovan."

Ray Donovan. For some inexplicable reason, the name sent a prickle along her nerve endings. Jason hadn't taken his eyes off her. When she didn't speak, he went on.

"Ray was a good guy, but he had a hot temper. He got into some trouble in the marines, and they booted him out. Frye scooped him up. At first he was glad to have a high-paying job. He'd come to see me and brag about how well he was doing. Then he realized what he'd gotten into and wanted to quit. Like your uncle. He went into hiding and asked me to help him turn himself in to the authorities. But it didn't work out the way he wanted.''

"The Sovereign tracked him down?" she asked, already sure of what the answer would be.

"Yes. Frye found him and had him killed. He makes an example of disloyal employees. Terminates them with extreme prejudice. That's his phrase. He didn't just take out Ray. He got his wife, Peg, too. And their baby."

Noel stared at Jason, shocked. She knew that it was true. Knew it in some basic, elemental way that forced a paralyzing wave of coldness into every cell of her body.

She wanted to flee from the terrible knowledge. But Jason's next words riveted her in place.

"He found out your uncle was planning to quit."

"My uncle had cancer!"

"Frye didn't care about his personal problems. Haven't you wondered why I came running into the jewelry shop right after the shooting? I was across the street videotaping everything in the store."

"What?"

"I was supposed to be getting evidence that your uncle was double-crossing the Sovereign. But I spent a long time thinking about it last night. I can't prove it, but the most likely scenario is that Frye sent those thugs to his shop to beat him up and murder him. He wanted it on tape so he could show obstreperous employees what happens when you try to give Sir Douglas Frye the boot."

Feeling as if the air had been knocked out of her lungs, Noel sank back into the chair. Jason was beside her then, hunkering down so he could pull her against him.

"Noel, I'd give anything if you hadn't been there. Seeing you on tape and knowing you were in the hospital—at his mercy—gave him the idea of using you as a courier."

She pressed her face into his shoulder.

"Last night, I was thinking about how dangerous this is for you. I can't demand that you risk your life."

She didn't move.

"I'm hoping you'll see this job through to the end. It's not fair to ask you to do it just for Ray and his wife and baby, but there are thousands of other people who have died because of Sir Douglas Frye. In chemical-plant explosions. And nasty little jungle wars. Or, if you can't deal with death and destruction on such a grand scale, think about your uncle. Maybe Frye was responsible for his violent death. Maybe that's just a coincidence. But there's Henry's whole life to consider. He wanted money, but it wasn't enough to compensate for a life of living hell."

Noel considered the choice Jason was giving her, considered the basis for a decision and felt a shiver go through her body. She raised her head and met his eyes. "There's still something you're not telling me."

She saw him swallow.

After a long moment he said, "When it's over, I'll tell you everything you want to know."

Nothing had changed. Yet everything had changed.

"I'll stay with you," Noel whispered.

"THIS PLACE LOOK OKAY?"

Noel peered out the car window, considering the unpretentious clapboard guest house on the fringes of central Brighton, a resort town on the south coast. The last place Montgomery's men would look for them, Jason had said.

They'd had four days of relative safety, where they'd spent almost every waking minute going over the images Sir Douglas had planted in Noel's head so that she could call them up without a moment's hesitation.

Tomorrow they were traveling north. And the danger would increase.

Although the guest house Jason gestured toward was called the Sea Side, it was actually a couple of blocks from the ocean. Noel didn't like the plastic geraniums in the window box, but there was an off-street parking lot.

She shrugged. What did it matter what the place was like? All she wanted to do was get out of the close confines of the car.

She sighed. "I guess."

"Help you, gov?" asked a man lounging on the porch when they climbed the steps.

"We're looking for a room en suite," Jason said in a cockney accent that made Noel blink. He'd told her Montgomery's men wouldn't expect them to head for a holiday area. He hadn't said part of his camouflage plan was to turn native.

"You and the missus? No kiddies?"

"Left 'em with their gran."

"I've got one private loo left. But only for tonight. We're booked for the weekend."

Although Jason pretended to be disappointed, Noel knew that a short stay fit in perfectly with his plans.

"Come on up and have a look, then."

The room had only one bed. Noel shot Jason a questioning glance, but he was already discussing checkout time.

The two men went back downstairs, and she was left staring at the double bed.

She'd kept her emotions under tight control all day. Now that she was alone, her defenses crumbled. All at once she had to steady her hand against the wall as scenes from her "honeymoon" with Jason began to jump in and out of her head like a travel agent's slide show. The opulent room. The view of the beach. She and Jason tangled together on the sheets, breath ragged, perspiration glistening on their skin.

Noel closed her eyes and tried to breathe deeply.

Jason picked that moment to walk back into the room, his duffel bag slung across his shoulder, her flight bag under his arm and her suitcase in his other hand. Slamming the door with his foot, he stood looking at her.

"What's wrong?"

Her eyes focused on him. "I've seen...you...standing like that...."

He set down the case with a thunk, his face hidden from her. "When?"

"Honeymoon," she said in a wavery voice, pressing stiff fingers against her flushed forehead. "The cabin... when we first got there. You brought the luggage in from the car." She blinked, confused. "No... it was the hotel on the beach. We didn't have a car."

Jason took a step toward her, his hand extended. "This is hard for you. What I've asked you to do."

She nodded, wanting to go into his arms but feeling so unsure of herself with him. At first, she'd felt so relieved to have the controller out of her head. But the more time she spent with Jason, the more difficult it got. The more confused she felt.

The room wasn't very large. Again her gaze collided with the bed. "We could have looked for someplace else so you wouldn't have to sleep in the chair again," she said.

He came closer, standing only inches away as he said softly, "You're almost letter-perfect when I drill you on the questions Frye will ask. But knowing the script isn't good enough. You're going to have to convince Sir Douglas that you're madly in love with your husband."

She swallowed hard, unable to meet his gaze.

"Is it so difficult to remember what it felt like?"

"No. It's not difficult at all. That's the problem. I'm so... my emotions are so confused."

He murmured her name, crossed the space that separated them and took her in his arms. She settled against him, closing her eyes and simply absorbing his scent and the familiar lines of his body the way she'd been wanting to do. It felt good. Totally right. Not some emotion engraved on a chip.

She felt his lips skimming her hair. All she had to do was lift her face, and her mouth would touch his. But she was afraid to put her feelings to the test. Or his.

He seemed to sense her uncertainty. Gently he shifted so that there were a few inches of space between them.

"We'd better go out and get something to eat."

"You like lamb shashlik," she said slowly, as a cozy picture of the two of them together in a dimly lit Greek restaurant drifted into her mind.

"Yes, I do. Did Frye put that into your Caribbean album?"

She shrugged, feeling confused.

"Let's see what the landlord can suggest."

Noel followed after Jason, still struggling with emotions that she couldn't sort out.

When Jason requested Greek food, they were directed to a small restaurant with red checkered tablecloths and

Greek folk music playing in the background. A booth in the rear gave them privacy.

"What else am I supposed to like?" Jason asked as they studied the menu.

She wished that for just a little while they could have a normal conversation without thinking about the implications of every word and every emotion. "Shrimp in spicy sauce," she mumbled.

"Okay, I'll have that for an appetizer. What do I drink with this kind of food?"

As if someone else were talking, she answered in a dreamy voice. "That night at your cousin's, the men were drinking—" Noel paused, trying to come up with the name of the potent licorice-flavored drink. "Ouzo."

"You had a sip and didn't like it," he murmured.

Noel stirred the spoon in the bowl of brown-sugar crystals on the table. "How do you know? You weren't there."

"Of course I—" He stopped abruptly.

"I wasn't there, either. It's just a memory someone else put in my head."

He stared at her for a moment, then gave her a smile. "But I was picturing you tasting it, picturing you wrinkling up your nose."

"I did. At least, that's what I remember." Noel lifted the spoon too high, and some of the sugar spilled on the tablecloth. "We're talking about it as if it really happened."

"Yes, and that's what we're going to keep doing, until it's the most natural thing in the world."

It was a welcome respite when the waiter came and took their orders.

"So what else do you know about me?" Jason asked when they were alone again. He stretched out his legs under the table, and one of his feet hit Noel's. As she automatically drew back, he gave her a long look. Then he deliberately stretched out the foot again until it was resting against the side of hers. Their flesh was separated by layers of cloth and leather, yet the contact was intimate. Neither one of them moved.

An instant later, Noel said in a rush of words, "Your father was in the merchant marines, and he was away more than he was home. Your mother didn't have any control over you, so she kicked you out of the house."

Jason cocked an eyebrow. "Is *that* one of Frye's little goodies?"

"I picked that up in the girls' room behind the cafeteria at school. A lot of girls used to talk about you. The ones who didn't date you used to wonder what it would be like to kiss you or spend an evening making out at the Westview Drive-In."

Jason snorted.

"Can you go all the way at a drive-in?" she asked in a strained voice.

"Yeah."

"You never took me there. Why did you take me out twice and then just drop me? Did you stop liking me so quickly?"

He cursed softly under his breath. "You've got it exactly backward. I wanted to make love to you, and I was pretty sure I could get you to say yes. But you weren't that kind of girl."

His gaze remained trained on her face. Flushing, she looked away and was relieved when the waiter brought their appetizers.

Jason cleared his throat. "There's something else you need to know. Sir Douglas's background check dug up the information that we went to the same school, but I told him we didn't know each other. He also knows about the incident at Mr. Dubinski's, but he doesn't know who came in and got the guy."

"What?"

"When he and I first talked about the shooting in the jewelry shop, I figured that it was safer for you if he thought we weren't connected."

"You took the chance of lying to Sir Douglas?"

"Yes. To keep you from getting involved."

"But you told me how dangerous that was."

"I didn't want him getting his clutches on you."

Noel stared at him and saw his face turn red.

"We'd better get our stories straight. It's all right for you to remember me. I guess I *was* one of Highland Town's celebrities. But it's more dangerous for you if he thinks I care about you."

She raised questioning blue eyes to his dark ones.

Jason reached across the table and took her hand. "He could threaten to hurt you—to keep me in line. I don't want to put that thought into his mind."

Noel looked down at her salad, waiting for words she desperately wanted to hear. He'd lied to try and keep her away from Frye. For old times' sake? Or what? Only the droning of the Greek music filled her ears.

Jason released her hand.

She curled her fingers around the water glass and took a quick sip.

"Do you understand the position I'm in?" he questioned.

Not trusting herself to speak, she nodded and began to push an olive around her plate. In due course, the appetizers were replaced by spicy kebabs and rice. But neither one of them ate much.

After Jason paid the bill, Noel stood up uncertainly, wishing fervently that they didn't have to go back to their cramped little room.

"Our friends have a make on our car. We need another one before we drive north," he said as he looked up and down the street.

"You look as if you're planning to steal one."

He laughed. "Hitting the motorway in a hot car isn't my idea of smart. But I've got something else in mind. Come on, let's drop in on the local pub."

It was called the White Stallion, and Jason started with a neat shot of whiskey, which he chased with a pint of bitter. Another pint followed.

Noel watched him uncertainly, wondering if he'd started to crack under the strain of the past few days. "Haven't you had enough?"

He laughed loudly. "Go on back to that gripe-water place we rented, if you like. I'm here on holiday, aren't I? And I'm going to have a good time."

His cockney putdown brought approving nods from the men at the bar. Jason scraped back his chair, left Noel languishing at their corner table and bought everybody a round.

Noel sat sipping warm bitters and thinking about slipping out the door and leaving him to find his own way back to the Sea Side. But the key was in his pocket.

So she watched Jason let his new mates draw him into a game of darts. At first he won and bet extravagantly on the outcome. Then he began to lose.

"I've got to save twenty quid for the landlord, but you might fancy the fine little machine outside at the curb."

Suddenly wise to his plans, Noel bit back a smile.

When the men came back, she stood up, put her hands on her hips and lifted her chin at a haughty angle. "You royal ass. How are we going to get back to London without our car?'' she asked in an imitation of the accent he'd been using.

Jason gave her a leer and patted her on the rump. "The wager is my wheels against his, love. Plus a nice little cash incentive.'' Turning abruptly, he picked up a handful of darts.

He lost the match with artful grace and mock chagrin. When the deed was done, they were the new owners of a battered but mechanically sound Granada.

The fellow who scooped up their car left soon after, probably afraid that the mark from London would come to his senses and demand redress.

Noel had enjoyed watching Jason's performance. She felt her tension mounting again as they made their way through the dimly lit streets. Jason didn't speak. And there wasn't enough light to see his face. But she sensed the tautness of his muscles as he turned the wheel and shifted gears.

Was someone following them? Noel swiveled to look. A set of headlights was closing in on them fast. But the car sped past and left them quickly behind.

Most of the lights at the Sea Side were out, and the car park was full when they returned to their lodging. So they left their new vehicle on the street.

Their host and a few guests were gathered around the TV in the lounge. Noel and Jason didn't speak as they skirted the group and went up the steps.

Jason turned the key in the lock. Then they were alone in the small bedroom.

He closed the door, but he didn't turn on the light. She stood facing him, seeing only his outline in the dim light from the streetlamp outside. But she knew how he would look, as she knew so many things about him, things that seemed to be more than the sum of the time they'd actually spent together—and more than the sum of the fantasy time, as well.

"Jason?"

"Noel, I drank a lot tonight."

"I noticed."

"It wasn't just so I could get that guy to trade cars. There's something I've known we had to talk about—before Castle Lockwood."

Chapter Twelve

Noel tensed.

"After I took the chip out, you were fighting me. Do you remember?"

"Yes." The acknowledgment was barely a whisper.

"Do you remember why?"

"I—"

"You thought I was someone named Gilmore."

She didn't speak.

He reached out for her, and she knew why he hadn't turned on the light. "Frye told me about him. I hoped to hell it wasn't true. But it was, wasn't it?"

"Yes."

"It was while you were alone in Baltimore."

"A couple of months after my mother died."

She heard him swallow. "I keep thinking that if I'd been there, it wouldn't have happened."

"Jason, don't torture yourself with what might have been. Sir Douglas is the only one who can go back and change the way things happened. And in this case, he did."

"What do you mean?"

Her vision had accustomed itself to the low light. When she tipped her head up, she could see his eyes intent upon her face. But the darkness was still around them, making it easier to finally say what she'd wanted to for days. "When you made love to me, it was wonderful. Everything I ever dreamed it would be."

"Oh, God, Noel."

"I did dream of you, you know," she continued in a soft voice. "Your cousin told me you were in the marines, so I knew you were straightening your life out. I used to weave fantasies about your coming back to Baltimore and marrying me."

"I spent a lot of time thinking about you, too."

"That night when we made love, the chip was in my head, and so were all the false memories."

"I'm sorry."

"No, don't be. After that night with—with Gilmore, I was afraid to get involved with anyone. Afraid I couldn't let another man put his hands on me. But, don't you see, when you touched me, Gilmore didn't exist. I didn't have to worry about my reactions. I didn't have to wonder what it would be like if I were with someone I cared about."

He stared down at her as if he could hardly believe what he was hearing. "Someone you cared about," he murmured.

"It was just you and me. And . . . and no nightmares from the past to haunt me."

"I've been feeling guilty about taking advantage of you."

The safe thing would be to simply accept his apology. But she couldn't leave it at that. "I've been feeling mortified about throwing myself at a stranger."

He stroked her hair back from her face. "Not exactly a stranger. And it wasn't the least bit one-sided."

"I've wanted to hear you say that."

"I've wanted to say it."

Emboldened by his response and the honesty in his voice, she went on. "I'm not trying to assign blame. And I'm not telling you my head is one hundred percent normal or that I know what we'll mean to each other when this is over. But right now, please don't let your feelings of guilt color the way you treat me."

He clasped her tightly, his arms a haven. "Noel, I promised myself I wouldn't take advantage of you again."

"I need you. I need your strength if I'm going to get through the next few days."

"I don't have the right to ask anything more of you."

"You don't have to ask for something that's freely given."

In the darkness, the texture of the encounter changed.

Nothing was really settled between them. But when his lips brushed back and forth against hers, they opened to him.

Her hands stole around his neck and shoulders, clasping him tightly, the way she'd been wanting to for days. And it felt so right. The way she'd known it would.

"God, I've been wanting you to hold me like this," he said in the uncanny way he had of echoing her thoughts.

One of his hands sifted through her hair, curling the strands around his fingers, sending prickles of sensation along the nerve endings of her scalp.

"I love your hair. I've always loved your hair," he murmured.

As he spoke, the other hand made a leisurely trip down her back, stopping to stroke the hollow of her waist and then slipping lower to splay across her bottom and draw her tight against his taut length.

Again she sensed that this was right. So achingly right. Her hands moved restlessly, touching him every place that she could reach, marveling at the way his body felt so familiar and yet so new. Every one of her senses was full of him. The tensile strength of his muscles, the scratchy rasp of his beard against her face, the dark, musky scent of aroused male.

And he seemed to be reacting in the same way—like a man relearning a lover's body and at the same time charting exciting new territory.

Before, there had been a dreamlike quality to the encounter. This was real. Herself and Jason.

His lips moved against hers, his teeth nibbled at her sensitized flesh, his tongue teased delicate tissue. As the intimacy of the kiss deepened, one hand slid around to cup her breast.

A little sound of pleasure welled up in her throat. It built into a moan as his fingertips found her hardened nipple. Wonderful. It felt wonderful. Better than before. Because now she was making a conscious choice to be with this man.

"Yes. Like that, sweetheart. Just like that. Let me know how much you want me."

She raised up on tiptoe, trying to align her body more perfectly with his. Now her hands moved urgently, hungrily, finding the hem of his rugby shirt so she could slip her fingers underneath and caress his bare skin.

A shudder rippled under her fingers.

Then he was reaching down to tug at the covers on the bed.

She blinked when he switched on the lamp beside the window. He turned back to her and cupped her face in his hands.

"This is really you. Not the woman who didn't have a choice," he whispered.

Again the words were so close an echo of her thoughts that she couldn't trust herself to speak. She only nodded gravely.

"I want the same thing you wanted last time. I want to see you. See your face when I come into you."

"Oh, Jason. Yes."

He took her down to the bed with him, and it began with whispered love words and hands that brushed like lapping flames. Heat danced over her skin, suffused her being, turned the core of her to molten desire.

"I want you to remember this, love."

She wanted that, too. The memory of the two of them together. True and real and vital.

And she wanted the same for him. She wanted to burn herself into his memory so that he could never forget her. Never leave her.

But she couldn't ask for that. She could only show him how she felt by returning his passion—and tenderness.

He covered her face and neck and breasts with soft, warm kisses even as his fingers stroked her most sensitive flesh, bringing her to a state of exquisite need.

She didn't have to tell him how aroused she was. He knew that, too. Knew how close he was to sending her over the edge.

His body pressed over hers, and she opened to him eagerly. They both murmured their pleasure as he entered her. He stared down at her, caressing her face, looking deep into her eyes as he began to move.

Then he was stroking her body with his, moving faster, taking her to a higher, shimmering level of sensation.

She looked up in wonder at his features, intense and changed by his possession of her. With a cry of gladness, she lifted to touch her lips to his. And then she was spinning out of control, crying out her rapture at the fierce peak of her pleasure. A moment later, it was his turn, and her joy was complete.

IN THE DARKNESS, something woke him from a light doze. A noise.

He tensed, his eyes probing the shadows of the room, but he detected no danger.

Noel stirred, and he nuzzled his lips against her cheek, marveling all over again at how it had been between them. His guard was down, and he let himself give in to the longing that hovered at the edge of his mind every moment he was with her. Against all odds, fate had brought them back to each other.

They had a few moments together. A few moments in a long, lonely lifetime. Was it possible to think farther than that? To think about the future?

Then the guilt came slamming back. Not for making love with her. It was clear how much they had both wanted—needed—that physical comfort. But for what was going to happen in a few days. He was taking her north—to Sir Douglas Frye's lair. There was no way that she could really comprehend the danger. Only he understood the risk they were both taking.

Adrenaline pumped through his system, and it was suddenly impossible to lie still. He looked at the lit dial of his watch on the bed stand. One o'clock.

He had missed another check-in with the Sovereign, although the arrangement was flexible if he had other business to take care of. Like getting a car Montgomery's men wouldn't recognize.

Quietly he slipped out of bed and stood looking down at Noel. She stirred and reached for him.

"Jason?"

He leaned down and softly kissed her cheek. "It's all right. I'll be back in a minute."

Trying not to disturb her further, he climbed back into his jeans and shirt. There was a phone in the front hall. He didn't have to say much. Only give his location and report that they were still in the clear. And maybe there would be some information about Montgomery's plans.

The crowd of watchers around the TV had long since gone to bed. Jason made his way past the darkened sitting room. After glancing over his shoulder, he picked up the telephone receiver in the hall and was momentarily surprised at the lack of a dial tone. Then he realized that someone else was already on the line. That must have been what wakened him. The phone ringing. About to replace the receiver, he stopped suddenly as a stray phrase leaped out from the conversation.

"Customs service."

Hand clenched around the cold plastic, Jason brought the instrument back to his ear.

"...checking out a tip on illegal materials coming in at channel ports."

"Bother." That was the proprietor responding.

"Sorry to inconvenience you, sir. But we need to question everyone at your establishment early in the morning."

"You've had these spot checks before, and you've never turned up anything at the Sea Side."

"There's always a first time, sir. Please don't alert your guests. Just set up for breakfast as usual."

Hoping the eavesdropping hadn't been detected, Jason carefully replaced the receiver and began to make his way quietly toward the stairs.

He was looking over his shoulder and didn't see the potted palm beside the newel post. The plant rocked as he collided with the stand, and his arms shot out, narrowly avoiding disaster.

A door opened at the end of the hall, and he pressed back into the shadows. The landlord came halfway down the hall, peering in the direction of the phone.

"Somebody there?"

Jason didn't move a muscle. Hours seemed to pass as he waited in the darkness, hardly breathing.

Then the door closed again, and he made his escape.

Noel smiled in her sleep.

They were walking hand in hand beside the shore of the lake. Then Jason whispered something in her ear and turned, leading her toward the cabin hidden behind a screen of trees.

They were going inside to make love.

No, they were going inside to—

She tried desperately to hang back, dragging her heels into the gravel of the path, because she knew what was coming.

The cabin began to grow and expand into Castle Lockwood.

The Castle Lockwood of her imagination. She had been here in her dreams before.

Sir Douglas Frye was coming toward her, a long, cruel knife clutched in his fist. He wanted the chip in her head. And when he found out it wasn't there, he was going to kill her.

Then Jason was between her and Frye, shielding her with his body, shoving her through a door. And the two of them were running down an endless, twisting stone corridor trying to get away.

She reached toward Jason. He grabbed her hand and held it tightly, and she knew that this time they were going to make it. She felt the tense knot in her chest begin to break apart. They were going to get away.

Then the world shimmered around them in a fiery explosion.

"Jason!"

She couldn't find his hand.

She reached frantically for him. But she had lost him in the terrible heat and the black smoke.

"Jason!"

Her eyes blinked open and stared at him as if she were looking at a ghost.

"Sweetheart. It's all right. It's only a dream."

"You . . . I couldn't find you . . . in the smoke."

"It's all right." He touched her hair, her face, her trembling lips. "I'm right here."

"Jason—" Her own hands gathered in handfuls of his shirt, and she pulled herself up, sliding her arms around his waist.

He rocked her gently, soothingly. "It's all right, love. You were just having a nightmare."

"I was so scared."

He held her tightly until her heart stopped pounding. "Better?"

"Yes."

He shifted her so that he could see her face. "Noel. Something's happened. We have to leave."

"What . . . what are you talking about?"

"I overheard the landlord and an inspector from the customs service. They're going to check the people registered here tomorrow."

"Oh, my God."

"It's all right. We're going to get out of here now."

He crooked his thumb and finger under her chin, turning her face toward him. "Are you okay? Can you get up and get dressed?"

She straightened. "Yes."

"I'm going to take the luggage out. Get your clothes on. Then come downstairs. I'll be at the front door with the car."

He left, and Noel picked up the skirt and sweater she'd been wearing earlier. Heart in her throat, she pulled on the clothes and snatched up her flight bag. She half expected someone to be standing in the hall blocking her exit. But the corridor was dark and silent. Minutes later, she scrambled into the car and they headed out of the city.

"Do you think Montgomery's men or customs tracked us down here?" Noel asked, leaning back against the seat, surprised that they had actually made good their escape.

"No. I think it's somebody's fishing expedition. But we can't take a chance on getting caught in the net."

She kept glancing in the side mirror until they were on the M27 heading west.

Jason cleared his throat. "I'm sorry I left you like that. What were you dreaming about?"

"The castle." She swallowed. "I keep worrying about what will happen when we get to the castle. And about the information I'm supposed to be carrying."

She heard him sigh in the darkness. "Maybe if I tell you a little more, you'll stop speculating in your sleep."

"Yes."

"All right. Frye thinks you're bringing him the formula for a synthetic fuel that could change the structure of world economic power. While he's busy auctioning it off, I'm going to take away his power base."

"Then who is Montgomery?" She asked another question that had been deviling her.

"He's a high-class thug who's been hired by one of the big oil companies. I don't know whether they want to keep the formula off the market or put it into production. But I do know Montgomery's intelligence network is better than Sir Douglas thought. He'd gone up against Frye before and struck out. This time it looks like he'll do anything to get the formula. And you and I can't put him off the scent by telling him it's false information. Sir Douglas would get wind of it."

"How are you planning to disable the Sovereign's power base?"

"It's safer if you don't know that."

Noel nodded in the darkness. "It would have been a lot safer for you if you'd left the chip in my head."

"I couldn't. Not when I could see what it was doing to you."

She reached out and covered his large hand with her small one, feeling his muscles contract under her palm. For long moments he held on to the wheel. Then he turned the hand over and clenched her fingers in a painful grip.

"When it's over, will you answer the rest of my questions?"

"I said I would. But what if you don't like the answers?"

"What if you let me decide."

"Don't think about when it's over. Think about getting through the next few days." His voice became businesslike. "I've been trying to give you breathing space. But I should tell you something about what to expect when we get to Frye's headquarters. You'd better count on microphones everywhere we go once we're inside. Probably also cameras. We won't be able to talk. So the first thing we'd better do is set up some codes and signals."

"All right."

He drilled her on clandestine communications as they drove on into the night, finally stopping at a small hotel outside Oxford.

Noel knew Jason was exhausted. But as she watched him sleep in the twin bed across from her, she was sure that a knock on the door would bring him to instant alertness, holding the gun he'd hidden under his pillow.

They were on the road again by eight, heading northwest toward Birmingham, where they found a charming B and B on the outskirts of a perfect picture-postcard village. But they didn't stop to enjoy the setting. As soon as they'd taken their luggage to their room, Jason cleared his throat. "Montgomery is looking for us up here. I'd better check in with Sir Douglas to find out what the opposition's up to."

"All right."

"I'll be back as soon as I can. Then we'll get to work again."

"THERE'S SOMETHING we have to talk about tonight," Jason said that evening as he stood at the sink, burning the papers they'd been using in their practice session.

Noel looked from the flames to his face. "What?"

"The ambush."

Noel clenched her hands in her lap. "I was hoping...you mean we really have to go through with that?"

"Yeah. Remember, I told you there might be a spy in the Sovereign's organization?"

"Yes."

"Well, Sir Douglas fingered him. Now he's using him to feed information to Montgomery."

"So he knows where we're supposed to be going?"

Jason nodded.

"But why do we have to go there? Maybe we got wind of danger and changed our plans."

"Sorry. Frye's had a lot of time to mull over the idea. He wants to make his chief rival think he's outfoxed him and then teach him a lesson he'll never forget."

"And he doesn't care how dangerous it is for us—for you?"

"He's betting I can handle it."

Noel looked down at her clenched hands. Jason didn't need any more problems—like a woman who was shaking in her shoes, for instance. "Well, if you can handle it, so can I," she said in a voice that sounded far steadier than she felt. "Where is it going to be?"

"A place called Kilmarnock."

"Kilmarnock," she repeated, with a shudder.

THE PLAN WAS TO ARRIVE at dusk, so they'd been driving steadily for the past few hours. They had passed a sign to Kilmarnock twenty minutes ago.

"How far is the house?" Noel asked.

"It's on this side of town. A few miles down the road."

Minutes later, they turned in between tall hedgerows. In one way, this was the time of greatest danger. If Montgomery's men scooped them up before they got inside, it was all over. So they'd worked out their arrival carefully.

In the gathering darkness, Noel felt her heart begin to pound. She didn't want to look to the left or right, trying to probe the shadows for ambushers. Instead she kept her gaze trained on the brick structure at the end of the driveway. It was a private residence, a bit larger than the first safe house that had almost become a death trap.

The place had a built-in garage. Jason activated the door with the automatic opener he'd picked up at a post office box in Sheffield. It operated so swiftly and silently that she was hardly aware it had opened. Before she had time to blink, they zipped inside. When the door closed, it barely missed the rear bumper.

Beside her, Jason let out a long sigh.

"Were you worried?" Noel asked.

"That was the tough part. We're going to have plenty of help now."

She hoped he was right.

Before they could enter the house itself, he checked in with the computer system by placing his hand on an odd grid-lined mirror near the connecting door. He'd briefed Noel on what to expect, so after the green light blinked on, she followed suit.

"Sentry defenses activated," an electronic voice announced. "Jason Zacharias, Noel Zacharias verification complete."

They stepped inside and a half-dozen lights on the first floor snapped on.

"How did it know who I was?"

"The Sovereign probably had somebody lift your fingerprints from something you touched. Maybe while you were in the hospital. He's very efficient."

Before or after they slipped the chip into my head? The scar tissue on Noel's incision tightened, and her hand reached toward the tender skin.

He caught her fingers and gave her a warning look.

She nodded tightly, taking a moment to draw in several deep breaths. Then her gaze flicked to the windows.

"With all the lights on, don't you think we'll be easy targets?"

"We want to make sure they know we've arrived. But you're right, it wouldn't be so good if they saw what we're doing." Jason went to the windows and pulled the blinds. Then, from behind a secret panel in the closet, he removed a machine gun, which he slung over his shoulder. Next he pocketed a revolver.

"Don't I get one, too?"

"Not if I can help it. The last time you had a gun was beginner's luck. Really, you're better off with one of the remote controllers for the house. Come on. In case you thought I was exaggerating, let me show you what this place can do."

She tried to match his bravado as she followed him into the living room, where he took a pair of hand-held controls out of an antique marble-topped chest. They looked a little like the one she used to change the channel on her television set. But although these were smaller—more like a credit-card-size calculator with miniaturized circuitry—they had a lot more functions. Jason had drawn her a picture of the keypad and had her practice some sequences. One number combination brought steel bars down over the windows. Another opened them. Still, it felt strange to be holding one of the devices in her hand.

She looked up to find him watching her.

"You'll do fine."

"Jason. Please—" When he'd grabbed her hand, he'd been reminding her that the cameras were recording the action. But surely needing him at this moment would be in character.

His face was expressionless, and she felt the bottom drop out of her stomach. Then he reached out and pulled her close. She melted against him, squeezing her eyes shut to block out everything but him.

"It's all right. It's going to be all right," he muttered.

She clung to him, breathing in his familiar scent, rubbing her cheek against the strong wall of his chest, wishing he could hold her like that forever. No. Wishing that the two of them could get back in the car and speed away and go somewhere Sir Douglas Frye would never find them. But it was doubtful that place existed. Even if it did, defeating the Sovereign meant too much to Jason. That was the real reason why she had come north with him.

She had signed on for the duration, and the most important thing she had to do now was make Jason believe that she wasn't going to fall apart when the rough stuff started.

Noel straightened and looked at the controller. "I'd like to practice some of the key sequences."

"Good idea."

They began to run through the house's bag of tricks. To the casual observer, the place was nothing more than a well-stocked country cottage. But the automated features built into the ceilings, wall and floors were an engineer's dream—or a madman's nightmare.

She was about to try deactivating the floor censors when the remote controller in Jason's hand sounded an alarm and flashed a red warning. "Intruder in rear quadrant."

Noel froze.

Jason's eyes scanned the living room and came back to Noel. "Are you okay?"

"Yes."

"Then get to your station. I'm going to check the back door."

Her station was behind the couch, a steel-reinforced barrier that would stop anything short of a mortar shell. Still, her heart kicked into overdrive as she sank to the floor.

Montgomery's men were here, and she suddenly felt like one of those paper targets on the FBI range. But the fear wasn't only for herself. She was relatively safe. Jason was the one in the most danger.

Noel's palm sweated on the controller as she listened for sounds of Jason from the kitchen. Instead she heard an ominous high-pitched hum. Then the bulletproof Plexiglas in the front windows began to vibrate.

She stared from the windows to the controller. Had she pushed something by mistake? The vibration was followed by a sudden crash of Plexiglas exploding into the room, as two figures in helmets and protective suits leaped through the barrier, scattering shards of glass like deadly missiles. As soon as the invaders were on solid ground, they began to spray the ceiling lights with bullets.

Chapter Thirteen

Shards of Plexiglas pinged into the walls. Noel flattened herself to the floor just as the room plunged into darkness. She'd gotten only a quick glimpse of the invaders, but she'd seen they were wearing padded suits that made them look as if they'd come from outer space.

"Halt! Unauthorized entry," the automatic sentry system droned. Moments later, a wailing alarm sounded.

One of the intruders swung around and aimed his machine gun at the control panel near the door, spraying it with a stream of bullets.

Noel stared in horror. They knew just where to shoot. What else did they know?

When the smoke cleared, the panel was sputtering and crackling. Noel held her breath. Had the bullets just taken out the house's whole defense setup?

A computerized voice answered the question. "System in red alert. Authorities have been summoned."

One of the invaders flung a curse in the direction of the ruined panel, his voice eerily distorted by the helmet he wore.

"Don't be a fool. It's a bluff," the other one interrupted in the same mechanical tone. "They don't want the coppers any more than we do."

Noel fought the fear that Montgomery had sent an invasion force of robots. But she knew damn well they were human or they wouldn't be so worried. Shifting the controller from hand to hand, she wiped her sweaty palm on her slacks. The fail-safe mechanism had kicked in. But where was Jason? He had the guns, but she didn't hear any shots. She had to clamp her teeth together to keep from calling out to him.

One of the men looked around the room and then back to the window. "For all I know, this place could be rigged to self-destruct."

"Then where the bleedin' hell are Zacharias and the girl?"

"Make sure your oxygen's working. I'm going to smoke 'em out," the distorted voice shot back.

Noel froze as she heard the hiss of a gas canister. Almost immediately, a heavy, acrid smell wafted toward her, and her eyes started to burn.

A wave of sick fear swept over her. For a moment it was impossible to think, as though the gas had seeped into the cells of her brain and paralyzed them. Then her hand squeezed around the plastic rectangle of the controller, and she felt a sharp corner dig into her palm. She'd forgotten she was holding the thing. But Jason had told her it was better than a gun. If she could remember the right codes. And work them in the dark.

The need to gasp in oxygen was a terrible pressure building inside her chest. Afraid she might black out, she strained to see the controller through a film of tears. Frantically she stabbed at a sequence of buttons she thought she remembered.

Music loud enough to wake the dead blared from speakers around the room.

"What the hell!" The startled exclamation came from one of the invaders.

Noel blinked to clear her vision. Music wasn't going to save her. But the floor in each room was designed to deliver a powerful electric shock. However, she couldn't turn it on unless she was protected.

Reaching around the side of the sofa, she tugged at a rubberized cushion and pulled it to the floor.

One of the space-suited men must have picked up the scuffling movement, perhaps with a directional mike.

"Over there!" he shouted, whirling and emptying a machine gun clip into the sofa. But the steel shielding held.

"Better have a look."

Noel's lungs were about to burst. As two pairs of booted feet clumped toward her, she scrambled onto the cushion and keyed in a different sequence of buttons.

Around her island of safety, the floor crackled and sparked.

Across the room, the invaders screamed. Then everything was silent. Turning off the current, she cautiously peered around the edge of the sofa. The two men lay unmoving on the floor.

Lungs on fire, Noel was forced to gasp in a draft of air. The fumes hit her, and she began to choke. Finally the spasm subsided.

As she wiped her burning eyes with the backs of her hands, she longed to suck in a deep breath. She didn't dare. Not until she was out of this room. But where was it safe to go? And where was Jason?

She began to make her way along the wall toward the back of the house, keeping her eye on the two men. Neither of them stirred.

She was concentrating on not coughing when she felt a large, solid body slide up beside her. Her scream was muffled by a large hand.

"It's me."

"Jason. Thank God. I didn't know if you were okay." With a choking little sob, she turned to him, pressing her face against his shoulder. He held her tightly for several frantic heartbeats, his lips moving against her hair.

Then he grasped her arm. "Got to get out of here."

"I thought by now we were supposed to have help."

"So did I."

"What happened to you?"

"A little scuffle in the kitchen." The sentence ended in a cough, and he tugged on her arm. "We need fresh air."

"Are we trapped?"

"No."

"You're wrong, mate. Raise your hands above your heads and turn around slowly." The order came from one of four men who stood like Darth Vader's shock troops just outside the shattered window. All of them were holding machine guns trained on Noel and Jason.

"Hands up, I said."

Noel complied. Jason looked as if he wanted to reach for the weapon slung over his shoulder.

"Jason, don't!"

"She's right. Go for the gun, and you're dead."

Jason uttered a low curse and raised his hands.

Satisfied that they had control of the situation, the suited figures stepped into the ruined room.

"You've run out of luck, Zacharias," the leader gloated.

Noel could feel tension coming in waves from Jason. His whole body was rigid, except for the thumb of his right hand. From the corner of her eye, she saw it move rapidly against the keypad hidden in his large palm.

Instantly, sprays of blinding white foam began to shoot from nozzles in the ceiling. He had activated the fire extinguishers.

Grabbing Noel, Jason pulled her down, just as bullets tore into the spot where they'd been standing. Foam rose up around them. Within seconds, the men by the window disappeared in a storm of white.

"Move!" Jason whispered into Noel's ear. She began to feel her way along the wall and lost her balance as she tumbled through the invisible doorway.

When she looked back into the room, there was nothing to see but foam rising like a wild surf. And nothing to hear but muffled exclamations and curses.

Jason clasped Noel's hand as they pounded down the hall. From somewhere above, she heard a motor. It grew louder, as if a plane was landing on the roof.

"Our transportation." Jason breathed a sigh of relief.

In the kitchen, two unconscious men lay on the floor. Jason hustled Noel past them and up the stairs to the second floor. He pressed a different set of buttons on the controller, and a glass wall slid open. Fresh air rushed into the room. Noel sucked in a grateful breath and then shivered as the cold wind cut through her foam-dampened clothing.

In the starless black sky, a helicopter hovered, a long ladder hanging from its open door, swaying in the wind from the blades.

Noel stared at it, sagging back against Jason. "I can't."

"Yes, you can! I'll be right behind you." He hoisted her up to the first rung. The ladder swayed like a vine in the wind. Somehow she managed to pull herself to the next rung, then the next. Finally she reached the open door of the machine, and a strong arm pulled her inside.

Breathing hard, she collapsed into the seat as the helicopter lifted off. Jason found a blanket and gently wrapped it around her. She closed her eyes and clutched the scratchy fabric, thankful for the escape yet afraid that the worst part was yet to come.

Out of the foam and into the Fryeing pan, she thought.

THE HELICOPTER DOORS opened. Jason gave Noel's hand a quick squeeze before shifting his grip to her elbow. She knew if she looked at him, her teeth might start to chatter. Or she might begin to scream and not be able to stop. So she kept her eyes on her feet.

In all the times she'd tried to prepare for this moment, she hadn't imagined it being like this. She felt fragmented. Disorganized.

Still dazed and shaking from their narrow escape, she looked from the intimidating gray walls of Castle Lockwood silhouetted against the night sky to the tall, slender man with the gold-headed walking stick who waited at the edge of the lighted landing pad.

Why hadn't Sir Douglas sent a squad of men to crush the invaders? Why hadn't the helicopter come sooner?

Anger rose inside her as the answer to the question came to her in a terrible flash of insight. The Sovereign had *wanted* it to happen like this. He *wanted* to see how little Mrs. Stepford Wife was going to react to her close brush with death. Once again, he'd taken advantage of an opportunity that had come his way.

So what should she do now? How should she play this scene? She struggled to make her mind function the way it would if it were operating under Frye's control.

Ducking to avoid the blades, she followed Jason toward the man she'd come so far to meet.

The infamous Sir Douglas Frye looked like nothing more than a nattily dressed country squire. Dressed in a Harris tweed jacket over a ribbed turtleneck and dark slacks, he appeared too fragile to carry the weight of the stories Jason had told her about him. And too benign.

She braced for his scrutiny, but he threw her another curve, turning the full focus of his attention on Jason.

"Well done, laddie. Well done. That jiggery pokery of yours worked perfectly. Montgomery's going to think twice before tryin' to mess me about again."

"I hope so. But I just thought of the basic plan," Jason demurred. "We couldn't have pulled it off without that house of yours."

"We'll share the credit, then. I'm just thankful we're on the same side."

The words were spoken with apparent sincerity. Yet there was an undertone in Frye's voice that sent a frisson down Noel's spine.

"Always," Jason responded easily.

"It's verra comforting to know that electronic bag of tricks works so well."

"How much of the technology have you transferred to the castle?"

"The bulk of it."

Jason grinned. "I should have known."

"Well, don't keep me waiting, lad. Introduce me to this gorgeous woman." The lord of the manor turned to Noel, treating her for the first time to the full force of his deep-set eyes. Perhaps it was the pale blue color that gave them an overlay of malevolent curiosity, but all at once she felt like a sideshow exhibit—the amazing woman with the computer chip. Only she was a fraud, and he was going to do more than demand his money back when he found out.

Jason threw an arm around Noel's shoulder, and she leaned into him. Then, with a nervous twitch of her hand, she brushed a damp strand of hair away from her face.

"Sir Douglas Frye. Noel Zacharias."

"My apologies that we couldn't arrange a safer arrival," the Sovereign said. "But I'm sure your husband explained about the criminals who have been trying to interfere with my business operations. Unfortunately, they decided to attack me through the two of you."

"Is it finally over? I want it to be over. I was frightened," she whispered.

"Of course you were, lass. Rest assured you're safe here with me. Everything is going to be splendid from now on."

She gave him a trembly smile. "Yes. Thank you."

As he stared into her eyes, she forgot to breathe. Then he held out his arms, and she commanded her body to move into them as if it were the most natural thing in the world.

She felt his strength as he crushed her against his wiry body. The hug might have passed for avuncular if it hadn't been a shade too familiar. "At last," he murmured.

"Oh, sir. I didn't really believe your castle would be like something out of a storybook. You don't know how special it is having you invite us here. Jason has been telling me stories all the way up north. But I just wasn't prepared . . ." She let the sentence trail off.

"I'd love to show you around. But I'm sure you'd like to wash up after your ordeal."

"Yes, I would."

Their host led them across a wide drawbridge and into the courtyard. Moments later, Noel heard a grinding sound and spun around. The massive wood-and-metal gate was rapidly closing. She and Jason were shut in. There was no going back. They must play this drama to the end—whatever the outcome.

Sir Douglas laughed when he saw the look of alarm she wasn't quick enough to mask. "Don't trouble yourself, lass. That stout barrier is just part of my security measures. They're even better than the ones you just encountered. They have to be. This stronghold guards some rare treasures. I'm sure Jason has told you that I make my money buying and selling anything of value. Ancient manuscripts. Prize horseflesh. Information."

"Yes."

"And what is the main source of my wealth?" he asked suddenly.

Noel was grateful that Jason had spent hours throwing her such questions. "Gems and jewelry," she answered as if she were accessing information from the chip.

"Quite right. Like the pieces you're bringing me. My men are picking up your luggage now." He patted her arm. "Which reminds me how remiss I've been. I was so sorry to hear about your uncle. He was one of my most faithful suppliers."

"I didn't know he worked for you. But Jason has explained it all to me."

"I'm sure so much new information must be a bit confusing."

"Oh, no. Everything's so clear—once I think about it," she said brightly.

She could tell the men were exchanging glances above her head.

"I'm so glad," the Sovereign replied.

"Jason warned me that the two of you would have business to discuss."

"Quite right, lass." Sir Douglas gestured with a barely discernible flick of his hand. From the shadows of the portcullis, two men came trotting forward. They were dressed in splendid scarlet-and-black livery that looked as if it had been copied from an eighteenth-century painting. But their physiques owed more to a twentieth-century weight room.

"Terrence. Kevin. This is Jason's wife. Be so good as to take care of her."

"Yes, sir," they both answered.

Two escorts. Did he think she was going to get lost? Noel wondered.

"You get some rest. I'll see you later," Jason said.

When the Sovereign and his lieutenant had departed, Noel looked questioningly at the two servants. They led her through towering doors into an entrance foyer that reminded her of the State House at Annapolis.

"Can you show me to my room?"

"Later. The Sovereign said you'd want to clean up first."

"I—I don't understand."

"We're to take you to the spa. You'll like the shower there. It sprays in all directions. And then Bridget will do your hair."

Noel felt her skin crawl, and she had to press her arms to her sides to keep from reaching toward the wound that Jason had reopened only a week ago. Last night he'd assured her it would pass inspection. Would it? "I'd—uh—rather get some sleep now—" she began.

One of the men took her arm. "Sovereign's orders."

"But—" Noel looked frantically in the direction where Jason and his employer had disappeared.

"Is there some problem? Shall I call Sir Douglas back?" Kevin asked.

"No. Please don't bother him." Unwilling to risk further protest, she let the men take her up a wide, curved staircase to a second-floor landing with a balcony overlooking the entrance foyer.

They made their way down a long hall and through double doors into what looked like a cross between a modern health club and a unisex beauty parlor.

As if she'd been listening for their arrival, a broad-shouldered blond woman wearing a crisp white coat came striding through double doors. The cheerful smile plastered on her face didn't quite reach her eyes.

"Mrs. Zacharias, I've been expecting you. I'm Bridget McKenna." She was large and strong, and when she shook hands, Noel had the definite sensation that if she'd wanted to, she could have crushed bones.

"Really, this is so kind of you. I know it must be past your regular hours. But I'm exhausted, and I wouldn't mind waiting until the morning."

"Oh, no bother. I'm getting paid overtime."

Terrence and Kevin took up sentry positions on either side of the entrance. There was nowhere to go except through the double doors with Bridget.

JASON LEANED back in a butter-soft leather chair. The room was entirely familiar. The Sovereign's private study. Floor-to-ceiling bookshelves lined one wall. Opposite them was a stone fireplace where oak logs flickered and burned.

Sir Douglas picked up a decanter of Scotch from the Victorian sideboard, poured some into a beautifully cut glass and added a dash of water. "How about you, laddie?"

"Not tonight, thanks." Jason crossed one leg over the other. "It's been a long day. Longer than I anticipated."

"Sorry our timing was a bit off."

Jason's voice held a hint of amusement. "Your timing is never off. You wanted to see how I handled the invasion force."

Sir Douglas nodded, his thin lips breaking into a grin. "Aye. I relish testing a man's wits. Even yours."

"I was half expecting it after you neglected to tell me about the chip in the girl's head."

"You never disappoint me, lad." He took a swallow of his Scotch. "Have you enjoyed her?"

"Well enough."

"Not a firecracker in bed?"

"A little inexperienced for my tastes." Jason wished he'd accepted the offer of a drink. He turned to face his employer. "I would have appreciated knowing you'd given her an implant before she started acting as if we were married."

"That would have spoiled the surprise. Besides, I couldn't be absolutely sure the technology would work. She's the first human subject we've fitted out with a full set of false data. What happened when we switched it on?"

"She was in a lot of pain. Then, as I told you, she got sick. Nauseated."

Sir Douglas swirled the liquid in his glass. "We'll have to work on that. It's better if the subject doesn't have a clue about the mind control."

"Mmm, I'm sure. But what if I'd handled it wrong?"

"As I said, you never disappoint me."

"Well, I guess my little wife will be glad to get some sleep after that show this evening. Which suite did you give us?"

"The two of you won't be needing a room together."

Jason felt his throat close. "Oh?"

"I had the lads take her to the spa. When she's all washed and shampooed, Bridget is going to remove the chip."

Jason didn't twitch a muscle, and he prayed his facial expression didn't betray the blood suddenly roaring in his ears. *Carefully. Do this carefully.* "I'm surprised. It's not like you to miss an opportunity."

"What do you mean, laddie?"

"You've gone this far with the experiment. And now here's your first mind-control subject delivered safe and sound to the castle. Don't you want to test the limits of her conditioning?" he asked in an astonishingly steady voice.

THE DOZEN HOT-WATER JETS felt good against Noel's battered skin. The scented soap and shampoo washed off the grime of the past few hours. But she couldn't relax and enjoy the experience.

From somewhere outside her wet, steamy world, she heard Bridget humming what sounded like a traditional Highland tune. Somehow the lively air set her teeth on edge.

The humming stopped.

"All done?"

Noel's body went rigid, and her eyes swung to the frosted-glass door. The woman stood outside the shower, a blurred, wavery shape.

"I said, are you finished? I really can't stay here all night."

A little while ago Bridget hadn't been worried about the time. Noel flattened her hand against the tile wall, wishing it had a secret panel leading to a hidden escape route.

"I've got to rinse out the conditioner," she called out, bending her head and soaking her already rinsed hair. When she knew she had delayed as long as she could, she shut off the water.

"Want me to hand you a towel?"

"No. I—I'd like some privacy," she replied.

Alone again, Noel snatched up the mint green towel waiting on the nearby bench and began to rub herself dry. Her heart was thumping as she quickly slipped into the terry robe and knotted the belt around her waist. She'd started across the dressing area when Bridget's broad shoulders blocked the doorway.

"Ah, I see you're ready. Let's go dry that pretty hair of yours."

Noel swallowed, fighting the impulse to flee.

"If you'll come into the ladies' salon, we'll get you fixed up."

"Thanks."

Noel wrapped her arms around her shoulders as she followed Bridget down the hall to a brightly lit room with a lone padded chair, two walls of mirrors and a rolling cart covered with a towel.

"Just have a seat, dear, and I'll be right with you."

"Where's the hair dryer?"

"In the cabinet. I'll just get it."

Noel stared at the chair. It wasn't facing either of the mirrors. In a beauty salon, didn't they always want you to see what they were doing? Circling the chair, she came to an abrupt halt beside the cart. Then her hand whipped out and snatched away the towel. Underneath was a row of gleaming surgical instruments.

SIR DOUGLAS SET down his drink on an inlaid table. "The limits of her conditioning," he said thoughtfully.

"I could write you a report, of course. But it would be much more interesting for you to press some of the buttons yourself. Get a feel for the kinds of things the implant can accomplish. And what it can't. How far will she trust me, after the ordeal at the house, for example? Tomorrow morning if I asked her to jump into that underground river that surfaces in the courtyard, do you think she'd do it?"

Jason could see he had Sir Douglas's full attention.

"Hmm. Your suggestion *is* tempting. Hands-on experience, as it were. But there's something I haven't told you yet. The circuits are only part of the chip." The Sovereign gave Jason a direct look. "The formula concealed in the jewelry is a decoy."

Jason pretended to be surprised. "Then where—?"

"I used a microdot. It's on the chip."

"You old devil. So that's why you were so worried about getting her here."

Sir Douglas grinned.

"I suppose you're anxious to have a look at the formula."

"Quite."

"But you trust the source of the information absolutely."

"Absolutely. It's sterling product."

Jason rubbed his chin thoughtfully, as if he were trying to work out an idea that had just formed in his mind. "And you're having an auction—when?"

"Day after tomorrow."

Jason steepled his hands, feeling unaccustomed dampness where his fingertips touched. In the long, painful hours of the night when he'd lain awake in the same room with Noel, he'd tried to come up with contingency plans. He discarded some of them as too dangerous to try. Now he found himself speaking words he'd told himself he'd never have to utter. "Imagine the drama if you asked Ms. Emery to serve as your hostess at the auction—like one of those pretty girls on a TV quiz show." He waited, letting the image take hold.

"Interesting idea, lad," the Sovereign murmured.

"Picture this. When the final bid is in, you open up her head and take out the information. Then you project the formula on a screen and the bidders all get their first look at the same time."

Sir Douglas tipped his head to one side as he looked admiringly at Jason. "You do have a flair for the dramatic, lad."

"I thought the idea might take your fancy."

"I could even give her to the lucky winner. Or better yet, auction her off, too. That way *I* won't have to worry about how to dispose of her."

Chapter Fourteen

Bridget was right behind her, so close that her breath stirred the hairs on Noel's neck. Her skin prickled all the way down her spine. Instinctively she tried to spring away, but the woman's strong hands came up to grasp her shoulders. "Time to get on with the main event."

Blood roared in Noel's ears. "No. Please—"

Something sharp pricked the side of her neck where an artery pulsed. Almost at once, her knees gave way and the steady hands shifted to keep her from slipping to the floor. Then she was being eased into the chair.

"Wh-wh—" Noel couldn't make her lips form the question. Nor would her eyes focus.

"Just relax. Don't fight the anesthetic." The voice was soothing—and deadly.

She tried to scream. No sound came from her throat. But she could still hear. The clink of metal against metal. Footsteps moving back and forth on the tile floor.

Her damp hair was just being swept to the side when, as if from far away, she heard an unfamiliar double ringing sound. A British telephone.

The hand left Noel's hair. Something small and metal clattered against a hard surface.

"Bridget McKenna here."

There was a short pause.

"No. I was just getting ready. Yes, sir. Of course, sir. I won't do anything further until you get here."

VOICES FAR AWAY. Talking about her. Only catch some of the words through the layers of fog that shrouded her brain.

"Does she know we're...?"

"No, sir... The drug..."

"And the incision is intact?"

"You may want to see for yourself."

Once again, fingers swept aside her hair and probed. "Yes. Good...opportunity to...the experiment...I only want her...partial consciousness..." Sir Douglas was talking about her as if she weren't there. Maybe she wasn't.

Another needle pricked Noel's flesh.

"How long do we have to wait?"

"A few minutes."

It was like the hospital. Her mind and body were separate. Far away...

"Noel?"

She didn't want to be here.

"Noel, lass, open your eyes."

She tried to hide from the commanding male voice.

"She's not responding to me," the Sovereign muttered. "You try it."

"Noel. It's Jason. Come back to me."

Jason.

He was calling to her again. Her name was like a rope around her waist, pulling her upward through layers of mist.

Finally her lids fluttered open. She was lying on her back. Three blurry images hovered above her. "Wha-wha . . . doing to . . . ?"

"You're in the beauty salon, lass." It was Frye who responded.

Noel's hand touched her hair. To her surprise, it was dry.

"Bridget was getting ready to give you a styling when you had a fainting spell."

Styling? With the metal instruments? Somehow she kept her eyes from swinging to the table that had held the tray.

"The chaos earlier must have been a bit too much for you."

Chaos

Noel felt as if a steel ball had been caught in her chest.

"Is she all right?"

"She may be reacting to the drug combination, Sir Douglas," Bridget spoke up.

But Noel barely heard her.

Chaos

The word echoed and reechoed in her mind. She shrank away from Sir Douglas. And from the frantic, clawing sensation inside her throat.

Jason. She wanted Jason.

She didn't know she'd said his name aloud until she felt his hand squeeze her. "I'm right here, angel."

Angel? Had he ever called her angel? On some deeply hidden level, the name registered. The cameras. The microphones. Everywhere. Not safe to talk.

Code words. They were going to use code words.

"Come on, angel. Wake up and talk to us."

"Jason."

They had practiced. Angel. What was that supposed to mean? She strained to remember.

Angel. Danger. Angel. Danger.

Her eyes came fully open and found Jason's. But their ebony depths gave nothing away.

"Sir Douglas was concerned when Bridget called to tell us what had happened," her husband continued.

Her husband. No. That was wrong. Jason wasn't her husband. That was from the chip. The memories on the chip. The ones she had to remember.

"Yes, lass," Frye said. "You gave us quite a fright."

"I—I'm sorry."

"Her color's coming back. Sit her up a bit."

From below the chair, a motor whirred, and then Noel felt herself being tipped to a more vertical angle.

She hadn't fainted. Bridget had been going to—

She pressed her hand against her forehead, praying it would all come clear.

"Dizzy?" the Sovereign asked solicitously.

"A little. I'm sorry. It's all too much."

Bridget handed her a glass of water, and she swallowed slowly, buying herself more time as her head cleared.

"Thank you. You can go now, Ms. McKenna. Please see that Mr. and Mrs. Zacharias's room is ready for them. The mauve suite."

"Yes, sir."

The room was silent except for the woman's retreating footsteps. Then the door closed, and Noel was alone with the two men. She could feel Sir Douglas's inquisitive eyes scrutinize her as if she were a specimen on a dissecting table. When he touched his hand to the skin just above the vee of her robe, she forced herself not to flinch.

"You're bruised. Is he rough with you in bed, lass?"

"No. I—I fell down a hill."

When she'd thought the truck driver was chasing her. But she wasn't supposed to remember him.

Her eyes swung to Jason. His lips were pressed tightly together, and his arms were folded across his chest. He couldn't help her.

"Aye, a rocky road to the castle. I hope it was worth it."

"Yes. Of course. Jason said I needed a vacation. After I was hit on the head."

"Yes. The unfortunate incident. How did you get out of the shop? Did someone come in and take you away?"

Jason. No. She mustn't tell. But her thoughts were like a tangle of string, all wound up together with false ends and knots. "Someone . . . I don't know who."

"A good samaritan, no doubt. Just like in Mr. Dubinski's grocery store." The Sovereign's voice was silky, hypnotic.

"Umm."

"You've led a charmed life."

It was so hard to think past the twisted threads winding through her brain, so hard to know if the right words were coming out of her mouth. It was only a matter of time before she made a mistake. "That's how I've felt since I married Jason."

"You love him?"

Noel swallowed. "Yes."

"Tell me what you like about him." The man leaned over her, his face intense and eager. She could smell the whiskey on his breath. "Tell me what you like best when he makes love to you."

The demand brought a flood of feelings. Needs. Desires. Longing.

"He's so sweet," she said.

Sir Douglas laughed. "Sweet!"

Her emotions were balanced on a razor's edge, and something in the mocking quality of the laughter cut her to the bone. She might have struggled for control. Instead she tore the wound open wide, invited—no, urged—the misery to build. Perhaps...perhaps that was the way out of the winding maze of this interrogation.

Tears began to leak out of her eyes and trickle down her cheeks. Then, suddenly, her body was shaking with sobs.

"Sorry... I'm sorry... please..."

"Get hold of yourself, lass!"

"I don't think she can," Jason cut in as he stepped forward and scooped her up into his arms. He cradled her against his chest as he stroked her hair.

She burrowed into his warmth, into the safety of his arms, but she couldn't stop crying.

The Sovereign spoke, his voice pitched low. But she heard. "How am I going to use her in the auction if she goes to pieces like this?"

"She hasn't before. But it's been a hell of a day. First the ambush. Then the escape. And the drugs. She doesn't know whether she's coming or going. Let me see if I can calm her down."

"Let's hope you can."

As Jason strode down the hall, his footsteps echoing on the stone floor, Noel sobbed into his chest. "Jason, I'm so sorry... I can't help..."

"Shh, angel. Shh."

Sir Douglas's gaze seemed to bore into the back of her head. Jason had told her that the only person the Sovereign cared about was himself. She'd believed it. But she hadn't felt it until he'd looked at her with the warmth of a snake about to swallow a cornered mouse. "Bridget was going to..."

"Angel!"

Angel. The name penetrated the fog clogging her mind. She closed her eyes, pressing her face against his shoulder. Microphones. Cameras. They were being watched. Everywhere.

"He said...'chaos.'"

She felt Jason's whole body jerk, his hands tighten around her. But his stride only broke for a fraction of a second.

With one hand, he opened a door. Then he was crossing a carpet and laying her on a wide canopy bed. Side curtains blocked her view of the room.

Suddenly he was gone.

She couldn't think. Only react. The room was hot. And it spun around her in a dizzy circle. The robe was too tight.

She tried to push herself up only to sprawl again. Thwarted, she began to claw at the fabric, pulling it away from her feverish skin, wiggling out of it until she was blessedly naked against the silk coverlet.

She heard Jason's indrawn breath and then a low curse as he set a glass of water down on the bedside table.

"It looks like there's only one way to settle you down," he said in an overly gruff voice.

He lifted her shoulders and hips as he yanked the coverlet down and pulled it over her naked body.

Next he stripped the knit shirt over his head and reached for the buckle of his pants. When he was naked, he began to move around the bed, pulling the curtains that hung at each vertical post.

Smothering darkness closed Noel in. "No...please..."

Then he was beside her on the bed, slipping under the covers, pulling her body against his.

"Settle down. Settle down and let me...come on, love, you know you like this." His voice was persuasive and loud. In the next moment, his lips were against her ear, and he spoke in the barest whisper, the words so faint they might have come from an apparition. "Get hold of yourself." But it was Jason, her Jason, holding her. As he spoke, his hands soothed over her shoulders and through her hair.

Noel closed her eyes, shutting out the blackness as she clung to the familiar hard planes of his body.

"That's right, honey." The loud voice again. "Mmm. You do like that."

"Feels good...." Her own words were a dreamy murmur, but she sensed the tangled knot of thoughts loosening in her mind. She knew what he was doing, and she was capable of helping.

He rocked her gently in his arms, his leg sliding back and forth across the sheets. By slow degrees, she felt the fear and tension melting out of her. He sensed the change. His lips were against her ear again. "Better?" he whispered.

She moved her cheek against his and felt him let out the breath he was holding.

"The chip? Do they know?" she whispered.

"No."

He stroked her lips. She kissed his fingers, opened her mouth, nibbled at his flesh.

Sir Douglas Frye had nearly driven her into sheer, blinding hysteria. But Jason had brought her back from the brink. A few moments ago Noel had hardly known where she was or what she was doing. All at once she was vividly aware that she and Jason were naked in a bed, their bodies pressed together. But just as she was assimilating that information, he moved away.

"Jason, come back."

She waited as the silent moment stretched. Then his lips found hers. But only his lips. He kissed her as if he was starving for her, strewing fevered kisses all over her face but always returning for long sips to her mouth.

In the dark, private world, the memory of everything they'd shared was there between them, around them, drawing them close.

Everything.

Fantasy and reality no longer mattered. There was only Jason, who meant more to her than anything else on earth. She reached to pull him back into her arms.

With a stifled groan, Jason moved back against her, unable to deny himself the contact. From the first time he'd kissed Noel, he'd known how much he wanted her, sensed that she could make a difference in his life. Back then he hadn't dared ask her to take a chance on a guy like him. Now he needed her more than he'd needed anything in his life.

"Please," she murmured against his mouth, driving him almost beyond endurance. Hungrily his lips moved over hers.

Her hand slid down, closing around his hard, distended flesh. Heat flashed through his body. In a moment he would be beyond thinking, beyond caring about anything but burying himself in her welcoming warmth.

But he had to be the one to think. He had to remember where they were and what kind of dangerous game they were playing. Her life—and his—might depend on exchanging vital information while they could.

He stole one last passionate kiss. Then his lips slid along her cheek and found her ear. "*Must* talk while we can."

For a moment, he wondered if she'd understood. She didn't move, and he heard his own harsh, ragged breathing in the darkness.

"Jason?" Her voice was breathy.

"Mmm. Angel." He moved her hand away from his burning flesh. Then, eyes closed, he pressed his head against her shoulder, sucking in deep drafts of air.

Beside him she sighed and nodded.

In the blackness, he tapped his finger against her palm. "Let's try something different this time."

"Something nice?"

The edge of disappointment in her voice made it difficult for him to get the next words out. "Very nice."

When he squeezed her hand, she squeezed back.

With his finger in her palm, he wrote a letter of the alphabet. The letter *C*. They had practiced this. Communicating. Writing messages if they thought they might be heard but not seen. Now, in the curtained darkness of this bed, exchanging information was more important than anything else.

She nodded again to let him know she understood.

"C-H-A-O-S?" He spelled out the rest of the word and added a question mark.

When she started to speak, he pressed his hand over her lips. "Not like that," he said for the benefit of the hidden microphones. Then with his mouth to her ear. "Don't dare say it. Heard it before?"

"In my mind." The answer was the barest whisper.

"After chip?" he spelled out.

He shifted, and his arm accidentally brushed her breast.

She sucked in a shaky breath he felt in every cell of his body.

For long moments, neither one of them moved. Then her lips were against his ear. After a sigh, she murmured, "In hospital."

He nodded, his cheek against hers.

"Means?"

"Code. I hope," he spelled.

In the darkness, Noel moved her lips against Jason's shoulder. The strain of writing out half the conversation a letter at a time, of rigid attention, of being so close to him and so aroused was almost too much.

She wanted it to be over. She wanted him to hold her, love her, make her believe that everything was going to be all right. But he was writing on her hand again. "Important."

"?"

"Media room," he wrote, and then continued in a whisper. "Hidden door. Escape route. Under third screen on right."

She didn't know what he was talking about, but he must think it was vital.

"Understand?" he breathed.

She nodded again.

He let go of her hand.

"Finished?" she mouthed against his ear.

"Yes."

Relief and desire flooded through her. "Then come to me now."

"You need sleep."

"No, I need you."

It was dark and concealing in the curtained bed. And like the eye of a hurricane, a momentary place of safety.

She heard him groan as he reached for her, felt his body shudder as her hot, needing flesh melted against his.

Her passion mingled with triumph. Somehow, his control had been the worst part. Now that control had snapped.

They were both kindled to flash point, yet they moved quietly, almost stealthily as they kissed and touched, totally tuned to each other but determined no one would invade their private world.

She forgot to be quiet when he entered her. But Jason reveled in her exclamation.

Then he began to move, and it was like making love underwater, the motions muffled and slow and silent.

The climb was long and lingering, prolonged almost beyond endurance.

Just when Noel thought she could take no more of the slow torture, she felt waves of sensation begin to crash and break around and through her. Once again she forgot where they were but Jason's lips covered hers, drank in her thankful cries. And she did the same for him.

"SHE HAD A RIGHT NICE figure under that bulky robe. Why did you close the curtains?"

Jason set down his coffee cup. "There's a limit to what I'm willing to contribute to your video library."

The Sovereign laughed. "The only way you've disappointed me, lad, is that I never could tempt you with perversions."

Jason reached for a piece of toast and began to spread it with wild blackberry jelly. "There's no accounting for tastes. But if you want her on tape, you can always invite the winner of the auction to spend the night."

"I've already considered that. Or perhaps it would be more rewarding to sell her separately."

Jason didn't look away from the Sovereign's steady regard. "Of course, she's yours to dispose of."

"I was worried that you might be getting attached."

"Constant adoration gets a bit boring," Jason tossed off. "But speaking of the auction, maybe you'd better bring me up to speed. Why take the risk of having them come here? Why not just do it on closed-circuit TV?"

"Because it *is* a risk. Or it would be, for any other man. This way I show the people who matter how solidly I've consolidated my power."

"Point taken." Jason set down his coffee cup. "I wish I could be in the auction gallery when they start bidding. But, of course, you don't want her simpering over her husband while you're dangling her in front of a group of other men. It spoils the effect."

"Quite right."

Jason steered the discussion to another topic. "Who's accepted your invitation?"

"Everyone except the admiral."

"I would have thought he'd jump at the chance."

"He knows me too well," Sir Douglas elaborated. "He's a wee bit afraid if he comes here, he'll leave in a tin-lined box. But Lloyd is taking the chance. And Buell. And Prince Abu."

"In person? Impressive."

"He wanted to send a cabinet minister. I told him he'd better get his royal arse to Scotland if he wanted to participate."

Jason laughed. "You didn't!"

"Well, not in those exact words. The only one who isn't coming in person is Spencer. He's too sick. But he's an old colleague from the CIA, so I've made a concession. He's sending his son Jed."

"You had the son checked out?"

"Of course."

They discussed the strengths and weaknesses of each man, and the plans for the auction. Finally the Sovereign leaned back in his chair.

"I can't finalize anything until I know how your little wife is doing. Go and take the lass up a breakfast tray. And have her down here in an hour. I want to see what kind of state she's in."

NOEL SNUGGLED deeper into the warm covers, smiling. She was dreaming about their honeymoon at the cabin.

She fought to cling to the good memories. Slowly they began to seep away. She pulled at the covers, tugging them up around her shoulders as if they could keep her safe, but she could sense tendrils of cold oozing into her cozy nest. Tendrils of fear reaching for her. Shaking her. Trying to wake her to reality.

"No," she moaned. Her eyes squeezed tighter shut. If she opened them, she wouldn't be at the cabin at all. The cabin was too long ago and far away.

Before—

She shuddered. If she let herself wake up, she'd be at Castle Lockwood. And her husband would be somewhere she could never reach him.

No. She wouldn't let it happen. But it was too late. The man she loved was gone from her. Forever. And the feeling of devastation was more than her anguished soul could bear.

A noise made her body jerk, and her eyes flew open.

Relief and amazement flooded through her. Jason was standing by the door, and she wanted to sob out her relief.

"Jason? Is it really you?"

For several heartbeats, he didn't move or speak. "Angel, Sir Douglas wants to know how you're feeling this morning."

His tone was offhand. His words were like a cold splash of reality hitting her in the face—reminding her exactly where the two of them were and why.

"I'm fine." She tipped her head to one side. "Last night was strange. I remember taking a shower, and then Bridget was going to do my hair. But I felt so woozy. I guess it was all too much."

Jason closed the door with his foot. He was dressed in dark slacks and a soft gray shirt. How long had he been up? And what time was it?

Their eyes locked as he crossed the room.

"But you were so sweet when you carried me to bed," she said, her vision going misty as she remembered their lovemaking.

"I aim to please." His eyes flicked away from her face as he crossed the carpet. "And so does Sir Douglas. He sent me to find out if you're up to a tour of the castle."

Noel sat up, pulling the covers up around her breasts. At least she'd drawn Jason's gaze back to herself. "I was hoping he'd offer." She was mildly surprised that the clenched feeling in her chest didn't show in her voice. Jason had tried to tell her how it would be when they arrived at the castle. She hadn't imagined it would be this bad. They couldn't really say what they wanted. No. It was worse than that. His face was so blank and his voice so impersonal that she didn't know what he was thinking.

Jason set the tray down across Noel's legs, then leaned over and kissed the edge of her hair. She closed her eyes, savoring the pressure of his cheek against hers, wanting to grip his arm but keeping her hands on the coverlet.

He didn't move for several seconds. "You're fantastic." Like the night before, the words were so low she could barely hear.

Some of the tension eased out of her body. "Thanks for bringing me breakfast in bed. This is so luxurious."

He stepped back and smiled, and she clung to the flicker of warmth. Then it was gone, and his voice turned impersonal again.

"Eat up. Then get dressed. I think you'll find everything you need in the dresser and the closet. Pick something pretty."

"I can't wait to see what's there."

"I'm sure you can take some of your favorites home."

Now it was she who couldn't meet his eyes. If she did, the fear and uncertainty were going to show. What were the odds of getting home?

NOEL HAD EXPECTED Jason to join her and Sir Douglas. But only the Sovereign's cold, appraising eyes followed her progress down the stairs.

She gave him what she hoped was a warm smile.

"You look lovely in blue, my dear." He gestured toward the graceful knit dress she'd chosen from the closet full of selections. It fit perfectly. No doubt they all would.

"Thank you."

"I hope you're recovered from yesterday. I was worried about you, lass."

She repeated the same assurance she'd given Jason. "I'm fine. I guess the strain of those men attacking us was just too much."

"Let me take you around. I don't often get to show my domain to visitors."

As Sir Douglas led her on a grand tour of his opulent home, Noel didn't have to pretend to gawk at marble- and onyx-inlaid floors, gold-leaf Renaissance ceilings, medieval tapestries—or the stream that had been channeled underground from the mountains and now provided clear, clean water for the castle.

"This place is more self-sufficient than an ancient fortress under siege. We have food in the storerooms and freezers for more than a year. And the fresh water, of course. If we locked ourselves in the underground shelter, I'm sure we could even survive anything but a direct nuclear strike."

"You must believe in being prepared."

"Verra true, lass," he said as he led her to his private art gallery.

Even as he played the affable host, he kept springing questions on Noel that made her skin crawl. She knew he was testing her mental stability and the abilities of the chip that was supposedly in her head.

"Verra good," he murmured as she parroted back word for word the false memory of Jason's coming to Baltimore after the shooting.

"Do I get to see your computer center?" she asked as they stepped out of the art gallery.

The Sovereign stopped short and gave her a sharp look. "How do you know about my computer center?"

"Why, weren't you and Jason talking about it when we arrived? At least, that's what I assumed. You said that all the special features in that house wh-where we were attacked are also in the castle. Aren't they run by a computer?"

"Quite right. But that part of the plant is off-limits to visitors."

"Oh."

"I do have something I think might interest you."

She waited.

"My jewelry collection. You are an expert in the field."

"I know a little," she replied modestly.

They had rounded a corner and Noel found that the route had taken them back to the main hall and that Jason was waiting for them. He had been leaning against the balustrade. As they approached, he straightened.

"Enjoy your tour?" he asked.

Noel wasn't sure whether the question was really for her, but she answered. "Oh, yes."

"I'm in need of a hostess for tomorrow afternoon," Sir Douglas said. "I hope you won't mind my borrowing your wife."

Noel turned to him, hardly needing to feign surprise. "A hostess?"

"At a little auction I'm conducting among some business associates. You'll be just the charming addition I was hoping to provide."

Her gaze shot to Jason. He was looking determinedly in the other direction.

Against her will, her eyes were drawn back to Sir Douglas. A smile flickered around his well-shaped lips— a smile that made her want to turn and run.

But there was nowhere in the maze of rooms she'd visited—or anywhere else in Castle Lockwood—where she could hide.

The Sovereign took her by the arm again. "Come along and have a look at my strong room."

Jason followed them down the hall to a stout metal door. The lock had a combination, which Sir Douglas quickly worked. Then he ushered them into what might have been a bank vault. Small locked doors lined the walls. A dark oak table and four chairs took up the center of the room.

"Please sit down."

Noel and Jason sat.

The Sovereign switched on bright overhead lights. Then he unlocked a drawer and brought out a wide bracelet studded with bloodred jewels.

"Antique garnets," she said.

"I see you know your stones. They match one of my favorite pieces."

He opened a small box, and Noel found herself staring at the locket that had cost Cindy her life.

Chapter Fifteen

Noel swallowed her gasp. She couldn't do much about the way the blood had drained out of her face.

"Do you recognize the piece?" Sir Douglas asked.

"Isn't it just like the one...the one I lent to my friend?"

"Yes. The twin. I was sorry I never got the other one back." He smiled at Noel. "It's been a long time. You have a good memory."

"I'll never forget," Noel managed.

"But you never knew the name of the man who came in and saved you?"

"No."

"Pity. I was hoping to jog your memory."

Across from her Jason hadn't moved. "Are we talking about the locket from the robbery in the grocery store?"

"Aye. I thought you'd like to see it."

Jason shrugged, picked up the necklace and swung it between his fingers. "I don't know much about jewelry. And, really, if you don't need me, I'd like to go down to the target range."

"Come back in half an hour. Your wife and I will be ready for lunch."

Jason nodded pleasantly, then stood and strolled out of the room. Noel somehow kept herself from calling him back. And somehow she kept herself from begging the Sovereign for more information about the locket. Had her uncle been using it to carry secrets? Had he left it with her for safekeeping? Had he pulled her into this danger-ous game all those years ago?

If she asked the questions that threatened to burst from her lips, she'd give herself away. So she kept silent—and continued to play the role of Stepford wife.

NOEL STUDIED the men who had been invited to the auc-tion. Arthur Lloyd, Clarence Buell, Prince Abu and Jed Spencer must all know about the chip that was supposed to be in her head. Why else would they be giving her such speculative glances?

Lloyd was a rotund British earl who looked as if he'd stepped out of a nineteenth-century painting. Clarence Buell was a bantam-size American businessman with a Texas accent. Abu was an Arab prince. His hawklike features were set off by a traditional burnoose and white robes. Jed Spencer seemed a bit out of place in the crowd. Younger and tougher than the rest, he was cocky enough to joke with his host.

She liked him the least. He'd held her hand too long when they'd been introduced. Then he'd crowded her as they'd stood talking at the hors d'oeuvres table.

The other men spent much of their time sizing each other up. Yet they gave very little away. The formula for the synthetic fuel must mean a great deal to all of them, or else why would they have traveled so far and to such a dangerous place to bid on it?

They had all come by private limousine direct from the Glasgow airport, although Noel suspected that the landing strip at the castle would have accommodated their private planes. But apparently the Sovereign had specified the means of arrival.

Another thing he'd demanded was that Noel look her best. She'd spent the morning on her own hair and makeup and then donned the dress he asked her to wear, a black sheath that hugged her hips. His taste in jewelry was impeccable, though, a diamond necklace and a matching bracelet.

Once again she looked toward the stone archway at the entrance to the reception hall. Kevin and Terrence flanked the door, and she knew other guards were stationed along the hall.

With a little shrug of defeat, she abandoned hope of seeing Jason. He'd done his best to avoid her over the past twenty-four hours. He hadn't been in bed when she'd finally fallen into a restless sleep the night before. And he'd been gone when she woke in the morning. Only the indentation of another head on the pillow told her that he'd been beside her at all.

He hadn't given her a clue about what was going to happen this afternoon. Not a word of warning about what to expect. He could have wakened her and done that in the dark hours of the night. But he'd chosen to cut off communication.

Panic tightened in her chest, and her fingers clenched the stem of a champagne glass. Had something gone terribly wrong? Did Jason know she wasn't going to make it out of the castle after all? Or that neither one of them would? Was that why he was distancing himself?

She struggled to keep her face from betraying her anxiety. Jason had convinced her to trust him and lured her here to Castle Lockwood. Had he only been using her?

"Well, gentlemen, perhaps we should adjourn to the media room," the Sovereign announced. He cut a very impressive figure in his tuxedo jacket and shirt over a black-and-red tartan kilt.

Striding over to Noel, he offered her his arm like a considerate host. As he led her across a palace-size Oriental rug, she felt as if she were being led to the gallows.

Unlike the rest of the castle, the media room was sleek and modern, with four swivel leather chairs clustered in the middle of the large space. The curved walls of the room held giant television screens.

Looking infinitely pleased with himself, the Sovereign escorted her to a tall, upright chair on a dais facing the bidders. All eyes were on her, and she shuddered.

Then, mercifully, he pressed a button on a controller in his hand, and the screens to her right and left sprang to life. A narrator began to talk of present fuel needs and oil reserves and projections into the future as pictures of jet planes, power plants and modern cities began to flash on the screens, interspersed with maps of the world showing dwindling oil reserves.

One screen shifted to the fires that had destroyed so much of the Kuwaiti oil fields, and Prince Abu muttered something under his breath. Then the narrator explained how a cheap synthetic fuel could change the balance of world power.

Sir Douglas pressed a button that stopped the show. "Well, gentlemen, now that I've whetted your appetite, let's begin the bidding."

"I want to see the formula before I pay for anything," the sheikh spoke up.

"So far, we're taking this on faith," Lloyd added.

"Hmm. Yes. The formula. Of course, I couldn't trust it to any sort of electronic transmission. So it was brought here on a microdot."

Noel tensed as the Sovereign swept his hand dramatically toward her. She started to scramble out of the chair. But Bridget, clad in her white lab coat, had materialized from a small door to her left. She pressed her hands firmly on Noel's shoulders, pushing her back into the seat. Then she worked a lever with her foot, and restraints came up to capture Noel's arms.

Struggling futilely against the bonds, Noel couldn't hold back a scream that echoed and reechoed in the cavernous room.

"You may know I like to conceal information in jewelry." The Sovereign came up behind Noel and unfastened her necklace. He held up the sparkling circlet. "However, the information isn't in here." With a secret smile, he corrected the impression he'd given as he set the necklace down on a table beside the chair. "The microdot is on the same chip that has been controlling our subject's behavior."

Exclamations filled the room, followed by new interest in the men's eyes.

"We're going to remove it now and project the formula onto one of the screens. Will that be satisfactory?"

Murmurs of agreement rose from the group. Noel stared at them in horror. She could see from the hard, bright looks on their faces that it would be useless to beg any of them to help her.

"Why don't we auction off the lady first?" The suggestion came from Jed Spencer, the young man who had been so forward with her. "That might be more interesting than getting right to the formula."

The Sovereign laughed and looked appreciatively at the speaker. "What a splendid idea. She's been here for several days, and my interest has already been stimulated. So you'll have to take her away from me. I'm going to start the bidding at ten thousand pounds," the Sovereign said.

"Fifteen thousand," Abu countered.

"Twenty." Buell joined the bidding.

"Twenty-five," Sir Douglas shot back. "Will anyone top twenty-five?"

Noel felt nausea rising in her throat. Just then there were several exclamations in the room. Parts of the media show were back. A city at night. A plane taking off.

She could see Sir Douglas was working the controller in his hand, but nothing happened except that the loud strains of a Highland jig filled the room, quickly rising to ear-splitting proportions.

"What the hell?" Spencer exclaimed.

"Just bear with me—" the Sovereign began.

He stopped in midsentence as a foot-high message in bold red letters flashed across the screen behind Noel.

DISK ERROR 999. DATA RELIABILITY SEVENTY-FIVE PERCENT AND DECREASING. The words were punctuated by a screech of bagpipes.

"What's that? Is it the formula?" Abu asked, standing up and glancing back toward the closed door.

"A computer malfunction," Sir Douglas said quickly. Noel could hear the calm veneer in his voice beginning to crack. Looking perplexed, he huddled above the controller in his hand, his fingers moving over the keys, but the action seemed to have no effect.

DATA RELIABILITY SEVENTY PERCENT AND DECREASING. HEAT SENSORS HIGH.

The Kuwaiti oil-field scene was back on one of the other panels. Only, as the filmed flames from an oil fire leaped toward the ceiling, real flames shot from the back projector.

Several of the men jumped up, backing away as smoke began to pour into the room.

In the next second, the automatic sprinkler system came on, dousing the air and all of the occupants in a torrent of water. It stopped as soon as the fire was out. Then giant fans began to clear the smoke. At least something was working.

Bridget dashed for the door through which she'd entered, found it locked and began to beat her fists against the barrier.

"We're trapped. It's a trick. He's going to kill us all," she sobbed.

Noel sat, stricken with terror, trying to make sense of what was happening. The room seemed to be going crazy around her.

Then, suddenly, she remembered their arrival at the castle. Jason had asked Sir Douglas a casual question about the computer system. Was it like the one in the ambush house? The Sovereign had smiled and nodded as he told him it was.

Jason. Hope leaped inside her chest. Was he taking advantage of the information he'd gleaned from the Scot and his own computer expertise?

With all her strength, she tried to pull herself out of the chair. Incredibly she heard a tearing noise. She pulled harder, and one of the arm straps came loose. Grabbing it, she peered at the torn end. It looked as if it had been cut part way through.

What about the other? With a little effort, she freed herself from that one, too.

AUTOMATIC RECOVERY FAILURE. DATA RELIABILITY SIXTY PERCENT AND DECREASING.

She was about to jump up, instead she forced herself to remain in the chair as she surveyed the room. The Sovereign was typing at a keyboard, shielded from the rest of the room by a glass wall.

Bridget had joined the men at the main entrance. Lloyd picked up a chair and smashed it against the barrier. Then he sat down heavily, gasping and clawing at his chest.

Abu pushed him out of the way and picked up the chair.

Now the message was auditory as well as visual. "DATA RELIABILITY FIFTY PERCENT AND DECREASING. WARNING SELF-DESTRUCT ALERT. SELF-DESTRUCT ALERT."

She had to get out of here!

Her gaze snapped to the TV screens as another memory came back to her. Jason...she could feel Jason holding her hand, writing in her palm. Telling her how to get out of the media room. Third screen from right. A door.

Noel stood up and stumbled down the step to the main floor. It was hard to move quickly in the tight dress. Reaching down, she wrenched apart one of the side seams.

The lights flickered. For several seconds the room was plunged into pitch-blackness.

One of the men shouted angrily and Bridget screamed.

Then emergency bulbs came on at intervals above the screens.

With a little prayer of gratitude, Noel began to make her way across the water-soaked rug toward the curved wall. She was almost there when strong hands captured her shoulders, jerking her to a halt.

Gasping, she tried to twist away.

"You're coming with me, lass," Sir Douglas Frye hissed. One hand twisted painfully in her long hair. The other kept a death grip on her arm.

"No!"

His face was very close to hers. His eyes were fierce. "It's Jason, isn't it? How did the two of you do it?"

Noel remained unresponsive.

"I watched him with you. It looked like he didn't give a damn about you. But he does, doesn't he? That's why I kept him away from you for the past twenty-four hours."

Noel's throat had closed, so that only a trickle of air was getting to her lungs. There was no way she could have spoken.

"Come on, lass. We don't have much time. How long have you been working with him? Did he tell you about the locket? That Henry never should have hidden it with you? That I wanted it back—and your friend got killed?"

Before Noel could absorb that revelation, Sir Douglas was speaking again and dragging her across the room. "Come along. If Jason knows I have you in the control room, I may be able to stop him."

She tried to dig her heels into the carpet, but he was far stronger than she. She couldn't stop him from pulling her back toward the center of the chamber.

Then a man was rushing toward them, throwing his solid body against Sir Douglas like a linebacker bringing down the ball carrier.

Taken completely by surprise, the Sovereign lay sprawled on the carpet.

Jed Spencer took Noel by the shoulders.

"What—?" The word was a strangled gasp as she tried to get away from this new enemy.

"Jason's friend—U.S. gov—"

"DATA RELIABILITY FORTY PERCENT AND DECREAS-ING."

"Jason did it! We've finally got the bastard!" Jed growled, looking down at the Sovereign's prone body. "He's finished without his information banks. The wolves will tear him to pieces."

All at once it was suffocatingly hot in the chamber. Steam began to rise from the rug.

"Quick! Didn't Jason tell you how to get out of here?"

Noel gestured toward the screen. "A secret door."

"Where?"

She pointed to one of the screens. "Underneath." Then she turned back to look at the Sovereign. He was gone.

Jed followed her gaze, swearing under his breath as he urged her forward. "We have to get out of here. Fast!"

They were almost there when a section of wall came away. Noel stopped in her tracks. Then Jason stepped through the opening. Noel stared at him, thinking her mind was playing tricks again.

"Noel. Thank God." His gaze swung to Jed. "I owe you one, buddy."

"Got to split. Frye's disappeared."

"Damn!" Jason grabbed Noel's hand. "That could be real bad news."

"Over there! A door." The shout came from Buell, who had seen the newcomer enter the room. Then everyone in the chamber was rushing toward them.

"No. None of you will escape." The Sovereign's voice—distorted and angry—boomed out of nowhere.

"What's he gonna do?" Jed asked.

"I took out his control room. He must have a secret backup."

Jason was tugging Noel toward the door when it happened. A loud concussion shook the room to its foundations just as a section of the wall blew away.

Jason flung himself at Noel, knocking her to the carpet.

In that instant a door opened in her brain like the door that had opened in the wall allowing Jason to step through. All the false memories. The honeymoon in the Caribbean. Jason Zacharias. Her husband. No, not like that. It had never been like that. As the room exploded around them, the truth exploded, too, like small time bombs in the cells of her brain. In that terrible instant, she *knew*.

"Jason! Jason!"

He didn't answer, he only dragged her through the opening and into a blessedly cool passageway.

She looked back. Jed was sprawled on the floor, his shirt shredded and his back bleeding. A line of flames was racing toward him.

Heart in her mouth, she watched Jason dash back into the chamber, grab the unconscious man and hoist him over his shoulder.

He staggered out into the passage again and slammed the door behind him.

"The others?"

"Down." He hustled her ahead of him along the passage. "Hurry."

Deep in the walls around them, she heard more explosions. Chunks of rock were falling to the floor. One narrowly missed her shoulder.

And then the voice of the Sovereign screamed his wrath as another concussion shook the castle to its very foundations. "You think you've defeated me, laddie. But *I'm* the one who will win. This castle is designed to self-destruct on my command. Didn't you know that, Jason? Jason, my *trusted* lieutenant. I've been watching you, laddie, waiting for you to make a mistake. Because I've always had the notion you were too good to be true. So I didn't tell you everything. You never knew about my duplicate control room, did you?''

The words echoed around them.

''He's gone crazy,'' Noel gasped out.

Jason didn't break his stride as he forced her to keep moving.

Jed groaned and lifted his head from Jason's shoulder. ''I can walk,'' he muttered.

''Forget it.''

''Didn't I give you enough power, laddie?'' the crazed voice echoed around them. ''Was that what you wanted? Or was it the damn girl? Was that why you turned on me?'' The Sovereign's voice had taken on a plaintive quality. ''Why didn't you tell me you wanted the lass? I would have let you keep her.''

They came to another door. This one stood open, and they emerged into one of the main reception areas. The wall hangings and draperies were on fire. As they watched, a section of ceiling gave way, mingling plaster with the smoke. Noel caught a glimpse of servants dashing down a corridor.

About to run toward the nearest window, she stopped short as she saw the glass was covered with a thick metal panel. The others were the same.

''Locked in.''

''We've still got a chance.'' Jason pointed toward a set of steps leading down.

The foundations of the building shook as they took the steps two at a time. Jason was beginning to stagger under Jed's weight.

He stood the man on his feet as they reached the underground river Sir Douglas had showed Noel so proudly.

Jed swayed and grasped Jason's shoulder. Then he shook his head as he peered at the fast-moving water.

"It has to have an outlet," Jason said, stripping off his shirt and slacks. After a brief hesitation, Jed began to do the same and ended up sitting down heavily on the worn stones. As he leaned over, Noel could see that the back of his shirt was soaked with blood.

"We can't . . . Jed can't . . . we don't know how far . . ." Noel heard the sick uncertainty in her own voice.

"Don't you understand? The Sovereign is bringing this place down with him."

Noel was staring numbly at the water when Jason stepped up behind her, grabbed the skirt of the dress and ripped it away, leaving her legs free.

"In! Take a deep breath. Then go with the current. It'll shoot you right out of here."

She gazed up at him.

"Jason, please. I *know*. I remember." Her fingers clutched his forearms. "The truth, Jason. I remember the *truth*."

The look of anguish on his face squeezed her heart. "You can't."

"But I do. Why didn't you tell me?"

He shook his head. "I couldn't."

Her grip on his arms tightened, but he shook his head once more. "I've got to help Jed."

"The hell you do!" the other man objected, trying to push himself up.

The building shook again. This time walls cracked and rocks began to fall around them.

"Noel, for God's sake! We'll be right behind you."

"Promise me!"

"I promise."

Before it was too late, she gulped in a deep draft of air. Then she plunged into the icy water.

The strong current grabbed her like a hurricane taking hold of a flower. She opened her eyes, but all she could see was blackness.

There was another explosion. She sensed it as a massive shock wave in the water while the river shot her along through an endless passage. She felt her lungs bursting, felt her grip on consciousness slipping, and she knew she couldn't hold out much longer. Then, when it seemed as if she would never emerge from the confines of the tunnel, light finally appeared above her head. Her legs were numb, but she forced them to work, kicking upward. Seconds later, she broke the surface and gulped in blessed air.

Somehow she maneuvered to the bank and managed to catch at stands of reeds to slow her progress. Finally she was out of the main current. Panting, she pulled herself onto dry ground. She lay there cold and shivering, looking back the way she'd come, straining her eyes for a glimpse of Jason. But he wasn't there.

She was alone on the bank.

Feet came thumping toward her. She looked up eagerly. Not Jason.

Just a man wearing a dark blue uniform.

"Miss Emery?"

"Mrs. Zacharias," she corrected, between chattering teeth. Somehow she had to hang on to that.

Chapter Sixteen

Her face was buried in a pillow damp from tears. Tears that flowed whenever she thought about losing Jason again. She'd begged the nurses to find out what had happened to him. But the staff knew nothing about a Jason Zacharias, or else they were trying to protect her from the bad news until she was strong enough to take it.

A terrible void had opened in her chest where her heart had been. Why had God given her back her true memories only to snatch away any chance at happiness?

The man she loved was gone. This time, forever. She fought the urge to withdraw. To send the awful, gnawing emptiness to some part of her mind where it couldn't hurt her.

Her hands clenched around the pillow. No, she wouldn't do that again, wouldn't take the coward's way out a second time. If she had nothing else left, at least this time she'd hold on to the memories of the precious week Sir Douglas Frye had given her with Jason.

The door opened and she tensed, waiting for the bad news. Then footsteps crossed the tile floor.

"Go away."

A hand gently touched her shoulder. She knew his touch.

"Jason!"

She rolled toward him, holding out her arms and feeling the tears begin to flow again. "I thought you were dead. Thank God, you're here!" It took a moment before she could continue. "Are you all right?"

"Yes."

When he still didn't move closer, she let her arms drop to her sides.

"I had to know you were safe." His voice was husky with emotion. He stood by the bed looking at her, and she could see the indecision in his eyes and new tension lines etched into his forehead.

Her eyes swept over him, taking in more details, assuring herself that he was really all right. Then she came back to the dark hair he hadn't bothered to comb. The guarded look in his ebony eyes. The hands clenched tightly at his sides. And she knew everything between them was far from settled.

"Oh, Jason. You're safe. What about Jed?"

"He made it, too."

"You saved him."

"He bought me the time I needed—with that suggestion the Sovereign auction you off first."

Noel closed her eyes. "I was so scared."

"I know. I saw the whole damn thing on a monitor while I was in Frye's control room taking care of his precious data. I'll never forget the look of horror on your face. But it had to be real, or Sir Douglas wouldn't have bought it."

"Maybe you think I don't understand, but I do." The few inches separating them were intolerable. "Come here," Noel whispered gently as if she were dealing with a wild creature that might flee.

He shook his head. "I lied to you. The whole time we've been together," he said in a voice that was barely under control. "Do you know how much I hated that?"

"You didn't lie. You just didn't tell me the whole truth—because you thought Frye would kill me if he found out."

The room was very quiet. Stretching out her hand, she laid it over one of his.

She heard a deep breath sigh out of him, felt his body shudder.

When he turned his hand over and knit his fingers with hers, she wanted to weep. "You remember when we went over the chronology of the manufactured memories?" she murmured.

He didn't move a muscle.

"Let's do it again. Only this time, let's talk about real life."

His face was agonized. "Noel, I've been paying for my mistakes for a long time."

"It wasn't a mistake! Just tell me what you think happened four years ago when you came home on leave from the marines. Why you decided it was all right to marry me and pretend it didn't happen."

It was out in the open. She had said it.

The bleak look in his eyes made her tighten her grip on his hand.

"Because when you lost your memory after the explosion, I knew that was the best thing that could have happened to you," he clipped out.

She shook her head. "Don't start at the end. Start at the beginning."

He cursed softly under his breath. "All right. Four years ago, I came back to Baltimore—and there you were. Just as lovely and appealing and sweet and giving as you'd always been. Suddenly I couldn't stand any more of the cold, comfortless life I'd been leading. So I asked you out again. And you were foolish enough to accept.''

Noel gave a little tug on his hand, and he came down beside her. She nuzzled her face against his shoulder. "Not foolish. All those years, I'd been hoping you'd come back for me."

"I was doing undercover work, but I was crazy enough to think I could have some kind of normal life. That you could stay in Baltimore and I could see you when it was safe.''

Sensing how hard it was for him to continue, Noel took up the story. "And we went to your cousin's restaurant. That part was real. What were you going to do if I talked to Frye about that?''

"Tell him you'd manufactured episodes to go with what was on the chip. I think he would have bought it, because he knew the process wasn't perfect. That's how the word *Chaos* got into your head. It must have come across the computer link when he was transferring data to the chip.'' Jason plowed on. "*Chaos* was one of Frye's favorite code words. I had a list of probable computer passwords that would let me into his system. You saved me from having to check every damn one.''

It was obvious that he'd rather give her details about Sir Douglas than talk about the two of them. Noel stroked her fingers against his. "Let's get back to us, okay? We'd got to the part about your cousin. He was so happy for us. And he threw that wild Greek party—with all the men smashing glasses on the floor and everybody drinking and dancing. But they agreed to keep it confidential, because they knew you were doing undercover work.''

"We got married the next morning at the courthouse."

"Then you took me off to western Maryland—to a cabin at Deep Creek Lake. We had such a wonderful week together."

"Yes."

"I started remembering some of it when Frye turned on the chip," she said softly.

The haunted look on his face made her heart turn over.

"God, what an irony," she murmured. "Somehow Frye stumbled on the truth."

"He had jungle instincts. He must have intuitively known the worst thing he could do to me."

She nodded almost imperceptibly. "The honeymoon at the lake was the one I wanted to remember."

While she'd been talking, Jason's grip on her hand had tightened painfully. She didn't try to ease the pressure. "I know why it ended," she whispered. "Peggy Donovan called and told you Ray was in big trouble and begged for your help."

"I had to—"

"Jason, I know. You're a man of deep loyalties. You had to help Ray. Just like you rushed back into that room to save Jed. But stop trying to help me."

"A woman who wants to stay married doesn't forget her marriage."

"Maybe she does, if that's safer than thinking she watched her husband die."

She saw the pain in Jason's eyes before he lowered his gaze from her.

"I remember it all—now. I thought *you* were in some kind of trouble. So I followed you to where Ray and Peg were hiding. When the house blew up, I was hit by the debris and knocked flat. Then I lifted my head from the ground and saw you stagger outside with your clothing in shreds and half your face cut to ribbons. Then you gasped and fell over." Her hand reached up and traced the faded scar on his cheek, drawing his eyes to hers again. "That's where this happened, wasn't it?"

"Yes."

She felt the syllable tremble through him. "God, Jason. I thought you were *dead*. Then I guess I blacked out."

"The doctors said you didn't remember what had happened," Jason said in a voice that was barely under control.

"And instead of letting me see you were all right and trying to help me get my memory back, you decided it was better if I didn't know!"

"Yeah. Because I knew I had to go after the man who had killed Ray and Peg—no matter what the personal cost. So staying with me could mean you'd end up like her."

"But your family knew about us. And what about our marriage license?"

"I told my relatives it didn't work out. That we'd got it annulled, and I'd tear apart anyone who ever mentioned it." He laughed harshly. "There's a certain advantage to being known as a tough guy. Then I got the record of our marriage pulled from the courthouse."

"You were very thorough. There was nothing left to prod my memory."

He nodded.

"I've been lying here thinking about why I blanked the man I love out of my life. I couldn't face your being dead. So my mind convinced me you'd never come back. I guess that's how my subconscious copes with the unthinkable. It tries to make the truth go away. Like after my uncle was shot.''

''This time was a little different. Probably you were the perfect subject for Frye, because you'd had a head injury once before.''

Noel nodded tightly.

''You're saying I was wrong to leave,'' Jason grated. ''But the past week just proves how right I was. My worst nightmare came true. Look what happened when you got mixed up with me again.''

He stood up, ignoring her outstretched hand.

''Yes, look what happened,'' Noel said. ''I didn't know about our past. I didn't know we were married. But I fell in love with you all over again! How can you stand there and tell me that wasn't meant to be?''

The stunned look on his face made her realize exactly what she'd said in desperation. ''Yes, it's true,'' she whispered. ''How many times do I have to prove I love you? That I need you?''

He moved then, hurling himself across the space that separated them, hauling her against his taut body, holding her as if his life depended on the contact.

''Oh, God. Noel. You're the best thing that ever happened to me—and I thought I had to give you up.''

''No. You have to make this marriage work.''

''I love you. God, how I love you.''

In his arms she felt his deep emotions. She felt passion and comfort—the comfort of memories they shared.

''Jason?''

''What?''

She moved far enough away so that she could hold up her left hand. ''Isn't this the wedding ring you gave me four years ago?''

''It was in my safe-deposit box. It was wonderful to see you wear it—and it hurt, too.''

Her vision was blurred by tears as she slipped the ring off and handed it to him. "Will you put it back on my finger? The way you did at the ceremony."

With hands that trembled, he filled her request. They gazed at each other, and she saw her joy reflected in his eyes.

As she gently stroked her fingers against his lips, he kissed the gold band.

"You don't know how much I wanted to tell you we really were married. Then when I sensed the true memories getting closer to the surface, I was terrified the Sovereign would find out how much you meant to me." Jason drew her back into his arms, kissing her with all the fervor of a new bridegroom affirming his love.

Noel looked toward the door and back at her husband. "Jason, I want to be alone with you. I want to get out of here."

"I want that, too. More than anything. But there's a whole crowd down the hall waiting to talk to us. Welby and some bigwigs from Scotland Yard, MI6, and the CIA."

Noel's eyes widened.

"Yeah. The Sovereign was numero uno on the international most-wanted list, only they couldn't touch him because he had damaging information on everybody."

Noel struggled to rein in needs and desires long denied. Then, unexpectedly, she giggled. "Are the bigwigs going to let me change out of this nightgown first?"

He joined her in the laughter. "Yeah. They've got some clothes for you." His expression turned sober again. "You know, you've committed yourself to an unemployed undercover agent, because there's no way I'm going to put you in danger ever again."

"Unemployed, hmm? Were you fibbing about getting a large sum of money for the Sovereign assignment?"

He laughed again, looking as if another burden had been lifted from his shoulders. "No. You're right. I guess I don't have to worry about a job for quite a while."

Her heart swelled as she heard the love and relief and the new note of freedom in his voice.

"Then maybe you can take me on an extended honeymoon."

"That, Mrs. Zacharias, can be arranged."

"And this one," she whispered before his lips captured hers, "I promise not to forget. Ever."

HARLEQUIN®

I N T R I G U E®

It looks like a charming old building near the Baltimore waterfront, but inside 43 Light Street lurks danger . . . and romance.

Labeled a "true master of intrigue" by reviewers, bestselling author Rebecca York continues her exciting series with CRADLE AND ALL, coming to you in July 1993.

It should be a time of joy for Abby and Steve, the hero and heroine of the first Light Street book, LIFE LINE, when their first child is born. But sinister forces from Steve's past come crashing in to turn that time of joy into a harrowing ordeal that has them fighting for their baby's life and their marriage.

Watch for #233 CRADLE AND ALL in July 1993, and all the upcoming 43 Light Street titles for top-notch romantic suspense.

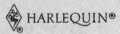

The most romantic day of the year is here! Escape into the exquisite world of love with MY VALENTINE 1993. What better way to celebrate Valentine's Day than with this very romantic, sensuous collection of four original short stories, written by some of Harlequin's most popular authors.

**ANNE STUART
JUDITH ARNOLD
ANNE McALLISTER
LINDA RANDALL WISDOM**

**THIS VALENTINE'S DAY, DISCOVER ROMANCE
WITH MY VALENTINE 1993**

Available in February wherever Harlequin Books are sold. VAL93

HARLEQUIN®

I N T R I G U E®

They say a cat has nine lives....

Caroline Burnes brings back Familiar, the clever
crime-solving cat, his second Harlequin Intrigue
coming next month:

#215 TOO FAMILIAR
by Caroline Burnes
February 1993

A night stalker was about to bring terror to a small
Tennessee town and Cassandra McBeth feared that her
nightmares would become tomorrow's headlines. Then
Familiar came to town with some uncanny abilities.

And be sure to watch for the third book in this
new ''FEAR FAMILIAR Mystery Series''—
THRICE FAMILIAR—coming to you in September,
from Harlequin Intrigue.

If you missed #134 FEAR FAMILIAR, which introduced this canny investigative creature, and
would like to order it, send your name, address, zip or postal code along with a check or money
order for $2.79 (do not send cash) plus 75¢ postage and handling ($1.00 in Canada) *for each
book ordered,* payable to Harlequin Reader Service, to:

In the U.S.	In Canada
3010 Walden Avenue	P.O. Box 609
P.O. Box 1325	Fort Erie, Ontario
Buffalo, NY 14269-1325	L2A 5X3

Please specify book title(s) with your order.
Canadian residents add applicable federal and provincial taxes.

FEAR1